REPORTER'S SENTRY

HUNT SECURITY, BOOK 4

JASMINE C. CALDWELL

Content Warnings

The Hunt Security series has an overarching plot and is best read in order.

This series deals with darker themes and may trigger some readers. Trigger warnings: human trafficking, homophobia, discussion of rape, use of guns and fists

She exposes secrets for a living. But her own could get her killed.

As a reporter for InVestigate Magazine, Violet has exposed some shady businesses. But nothing has ever tipped her journalist radar quite like the mystery of Nautical Transit. No matter what she does, she can't get them to talk to her. But Violet's never given up on a lead. What would her idol, Nellie Bly, do?

Sick of the politics in Annapolis, Jon retires from the Navy and goes home to Baltimore to work for his brother. Hunt Security offers him both excitement and the family connection he's been missing. When an editor at InVestigate Magazine reaches out about her best reporter disappearing, Jon realizes the missing woman is the one he fell for years ago—the one that got away. Now he's going undercover at the syndicate's shell company, Nautical Transit, to discover what happened to Violet.

Did Violet finally bite off more than she can chew? And what will Jon find when he goes searching for the truth?

PART I

Chapter 1

Her heels clicked against the cement, or what was left of it. The dimly lit parking lot made walking without twisting an ankle difficult. But Violet Giordano needed to maintain appearances for her character of Ramona, a bombshell and the Rusty Nail Saloon's newest waitress.

Violet had been with InVestigate Magazine for a year in the business division. Their articles exposed shady business practices. It ended up being a lot of white-collar crime, easily discovered through paper trails and interviews with disgruntled ex-employees. But this had been a different type of tip in the anonymous suggestion box.

A mother claimed her son had overdosed on heroin, and on his deathbed admitted he'd purchased the drugs from the back of the Rusty Nail. She'd gone to the cops, but without having witnessed the sale herself, there wasn't anything they could do. Annapolis police were spread as thin as any metropolitan force in the country. And a distraught mother grieving for her son without evidence to back up her claim didn't register high enough on the force's list of priorities. His death had been lumped in with other statistics and the investigation went nowhere.

So, the mom had turned to InVestigate to prove her son's final words were true, and to get justice for him.

As the newest member of the team, Violet had been thrilled when Wanda assigned her this story. She'd gone through the normal routes; but the problem was that the former employees of this dive bar hadn't wanted to talk. Whether it was because they didn't know anything or they were afraid to snitch, she wasn't sure. In the end, she'd applied for a waitress job under a fake name. She'd even spent her own money for false identification papers. To say Wanda was less than thrilled at this decision would be an understatement.

But Violet felt there was no other way to get her answers. For a dive bar, it was awfully well secured. She'd discovered a high-end security system on her early reconnaissance trip, which had been something else that tripped her Spidey-senses. The Rusty Nail stood in one of the poorer areas of Annapolis, Maryland. Hardly the type of place one would expect to find such an expensive piece of technology.

What were they hiding?

She clocked in at the ancient punch clock in the back of the kitchen and shoved her purse with her fake ID in the cubby with her alter ego's name on it. Then she propped her small but perky boobs further up in her skin-tight black tank top with the crisscrossing straps down her back.

"Girl, you're going to be raking in the tips tonight." A voice behind her made her turn. Chloe, one of the other servers, stood at the punch clock.

Violet snorted. "Hardly. I might if I had your tits." Chloe had curves for days, a fact Violet would have been envious of in her younger years.

"Ha! If I wore something like that, I'd take out someone's eye!"

"And they'd pay you for the privilege." Chloe responded by laughing with her, their camaraderie easy.

It was all an act, of course. Once Violet had what she needed, she'd never see or speak to these people again.

Back in grade school, Violet wrote a report on Nellie Bly, arguably the first female investigative reporter. She'd read about her going undercover as a factory worker, and naturally, her exposé of the New York Asylum that brought about mental health reform and made her famous. When her usual methods led to dead ends, she'd asked herself, "What would Nellie do?"

And that's how she ended up here.

The night went by quickly. Violet's tables kept her hopping, but she was hyper aware of what the manager, Ray, was doing. Or rather, what he wasn't doing.

Once things got busy on the weekends, he always slipped away to the office. Except if you actually needed something and went back to his office, it'd be locked and dark.

Violet suspected he was in the store room, managing his *other* business. But until she got a break, she wouldn't be able to sneak back there to see for herself.

Standing at the bar, waiting for the bartender on duty to fucking notice her already so she could get this order to her table, she sensed a presence behind her, and spun around to spy a tall man whose black t-shirt barely contained his muscles, with a short military-style haircut and green eyes that sparkled when he caught sight of her.

"Hello there," she said, her charm turned up to eleven as she leaned back against the bar. Could he be a bouncer? Or maybe someone else who worked here that she could pump for information? She'd only been working there for two weeks and didn't know everyone yet.

"Can I buy you a drink?"

Not an employee, then. Hmm. She had to give him credit; he didn't look away from her face. "Sorry, honey, I'm working."

"What time do you get off?"

Violet snickered at the wild comments that ran through her head, full of innuendo. "I'm closing tonight."

"Come find me when you're done." He winked, then glanced at her name tag. "If you're not too tired, that is, Ramona."

Alright, then. There was no rule about a one-night stand with a hot patron. For a guy as hot as this one, she could definitely keep up her ruse a little after closing time.

"What's your name?"

"I'm Jon. Short for Jonathon."

"I'll see you around then, Jon." Finally, her drinks were ready, and she lifted the tray to her shoulder and marched back to her tables.

She caught sight of him several times the rest of her shift. He played a couple rounds of darts with some regulars, then he sat at the bar and nursed a beer for the night. Chloe even noticed.

"You caught someone's eye tonight, girlie."

Violet shrugged. "He wanted to buy me a drink, but I told him I was working."

"He doesn't usually stay this long," she commented as they put the cleared glasses into the bin for the dishwasher.

"Does he come around a lot?"

"Every so often." Chloe shrugged. "He's not a regular, but he's here enough. And hot as hell, too."

"I know."

"Is he hanging around for you?"

"Maybe."

Chloe nudged her terra cotta shoulder against Violet's pale one. "Get you some. I wouldn't kick that man out of bed for eating crackers."

Violet's cheeks heated, but she grinned. Then a thought occurred to her. It'd be best not to be too memorable to her coworkers. And nothing stuck in one's memory better than scandal. "Ray won't have a problem?"

"What Ray don't know won't hurt him. It's only an issue if the customer makes it one." Chloe winked. "I got your back, girlie."

"Thanks." They bumped shoulders again.

"It's time for my break," Chloe said. "You want a smoke?"

"Nah, not my thing. I have to run to the ladies' room."

"Alright, see you back out there."

Violet waited until Chloe was out of sight, heading toward the smoking area for the employees behind the building. Then she jetted off in the direction of the bathroom, but veered off and headed down the hall to the storage room.

Anyone would think that room would be used regularly during these business hours. But anything the front of the house could run out of was stored in a closet next to the office. Violet literally had no excuse to get into that room. But she could go down the hallway without rousing too much suspicion.

Carefully, she peeled the adhesive backing off the tiny spy cameras she'd purchased online. One went onto the picture frame, angled so it faced the door. The other went above the solid door to watch as people came and went. She'd have to come back during a daylight shift with her lock pick when the storage room was empty to place the third camera. But this would do for now. Hopefully someone would mess up and her cameras would be there to catch it.

She took quick steps on the balls of her feet to quiet her heels and backtracked to the bathroom. There she did her business and washed her hands, then touched up the eyeliner that had smudged a bit over the course of her shift. Only a couple of hours left. Would Hot Stuff still be hanging around? Or would he have gotten tired of waiting and left?

When she went back out, the bartender was making the last call announcement. And Jon was still sitting at the bar, sipping at a glass of what appeared to be water. He winked at her, and she returned to work.

She had to fight her nerves down the closer it got to closing time. It had been a while since she'd been laid, and she desperately wanted to take him for a ride. When the clock switched over and the bouncers started kicking patrons out, she noticed Jon wasn't among them.

"Hey Ramona, I didn't know you had a boyfriend." Jamal, one of the bouncers, said as they stood in line to punch out.

"What?"

"That dude out there said he's waiting for you."

"Yeah, no, he's uh... just my date."

Jamal grunted. "I told him he could wait inside this time, but he's gotta go with you, okay?"

"No problem, Jamal. Thanks." She patted his arm and slung her purse over her shoulder, then hurried down the hallway for the front door, where Jon stood.

"You hungry?"

"Sure." She could eat a horse, but she also had food back at the apartment. However, if the man wanted to buy her dinner, she wouldn't turn him down.

"Great. There's a twenty-four-hour place not too far from here. You want to follow me?"

"Sounds good."

Jon walked her to her car, then pointed out his truck, a big red pickup at the other end of the parking lot. "If you get lost, it's Sally's Diner."

"Okay, great." She slipped out of her heels and into the flats she kept in the car. After six hours on her feet, her poor arches needed a break.

She followed him down to the small retro diner. She'd been past it before, but never had a reason to go inside the silver bullet-shaped building. Tiny was the best word to describe it, followed by stereotypical. An abundance of shiny chrome, red vinyl, and a checkerboard floor, along with a jukebox in the corner that looked like it had been there since the fifties. The sign said "Seat Yourself" and since there were only a couple of other tables with anyone there, it was easy for the server to come over and hand them menus.

After deciding on a greasy burger and fries, Violet lowered her menu to see Jon's green eyes on her. "How'd a nice girl like you end up working at a joint like that?"

She shrugged. "I needed money. If it's so shady, what are you doing there?"

He grinned. "Avoiding my boss."

The server came back around and they placed their orders. She got her burger and fries; he ordered the Philly cheesesteak and onion rings.

"Tell me about yourself, Jon."

She learned he was the second oldest of four who had gone into the Navy after high school. Both of his brothers were in other branches of the military, the oldest was in the Army and the younger one had joined the Marines. The youngest was a girl, and Violet pitied her trying to date.

"How about you? Are you in school?"

Violet snorted. How old did he think she was? "Nah, not for me. I'm just trying to get by." She couldn't exactly explain she'd already graduated years ago.

"I've never met a Ramona before. Where'd your parents get the name?"

She giggled. "It's actually a book character. Mom read me all her favorite books growing up." Not a lie. She'd loved Beverly Cleary's series growing up and her mother had read them all to her. And yes, that's why she'd picked this name for this investigation. But she needed to get him talking about himself.

"What's it like in the Navy?"

He couldn't tell her exactly what his job was, but he told her funny stories of life on a submarine and later an aircraft carrier.

Her goal had been to get him into bed. But when they finished their pie, and he paid the check, all he did was walk her to her car.

Violet leaned against her sedan, stars twinkling above their heads. "You wanna come back to my place?"

Jon licked his lips, then one hand left his pocket and tucked a stray piece of her dark hair behind her ear. "Not tonight, sweetheart. Or this morning, rather." Then he leaned in and hovered over her mouth, breathing in the air she exhaled. Her lips tingled at his closeness. "I gotta get some sleep for work. But if you give me your number, we can do this again."

Butterflies erupted in her stomach. "I work a lot," she responded breathily.

He grinned. "That's okay. I'll know where to find you, then." Then he took out his phone and unlocked it. "Put your number in it."

She did as she was told, then watched him save it and text her. Her phone buzzed in her purse. "There, now you have mine." He leaned forward once more and gently touched her nose with his. His voice dropped almost to a whisper. "Can I kiss you, Ramona?"

"Ye-yeah." Who was she? Was she acting as Violet or Ramona? And why did she care?

His lips met hers in a gentle exploration, his tongue taking advantage of her gasp. He tasted like the cherry pie he'd eaten in the diner. Violet moaned as their tongues tangled and he grabbed onto her and gripped her tight. His hands covered her ass entirely, and she moaned again thinking about how he could man handle her in the bedroom. It was always such a turn on when a guy could pick her up.

Eventually, he pulled back and let her breathe, setting her back on the ground. "I'll see you soon."

"I sure hope so, sailor."

Chapter 2

"Hey Hunt, a bunch of us are meeting at the officer's club tonight for drinks. You should come."

Lieutenant Jonathon Hunt looked up from the report on his desk. "Sorry, I have plans already."

"Suit yourself. You'll be at the barbecue on Sunday?"

"Yeah, I'll be there." Jon wrapped up what he was doing and sent it off to his superior officer, then shut down his computer for the night. The pace of this desk job was slower than he was used to, but staying on land helped ease his mother's mind. This way, one of her boys stayed out of danger. Though he knew Roger was getting close to having his twenty years in and wanted to retire, Jon was happy to make the sacrifice. Living on submarines hadn't been his idea of a good time.

He waved at the coworkers whose names he hadn't had time to learn yet and strode out to his truck in the Maryland summer sun. Ramona was working tonight and he couldn't wait to get to the Rusty Nail.

Ever since that kiss outside Sally's two weeks ago, he'd had her on his mind. He'd been back every night she mentioned she worked, since that was one of the few ways he could see her. Ramona barely responded to his texts and wouldn't agree to meet him outside of the bar. She closed almost every night, so he hadn't been able to stay late on work nights. But last Friday he'd taken her back to the all-night diner for another date.

He didn't know what it was, but her attempts to resist him made him want her that much more.

With a quick change into his civilian clothes, Jon was off to The Rusty Nail Saloon. He showed his ID to the bouncer and found what he was starting to consider his booth at the back open and waiting for him. Sure enough, Ramona walked through the kitchen doors. Those painted on jeans taunted him with that perfect ass that fit so nicely in his hands. And her luscious, mouth-sized breasts peeked up from her black tank top. This one was slightly more casual than the first one she'd worn, but Jon liked her in anything.

"Hey Navy boy, how are you?"

"Better now that you're here," he replied with his most charming grin. A faint pink blush stole over her cheeks as she approached.

"What can I get you?"

"This is your section tonight?"

"Sailor, any section you're in is my section."

"You claiming me, Mona?" Fuck, that idea was hot.

A slow, sly grin spread across her plump lips as she leaned in. "Maybe I am."

He slid closer to the edge to whisper in her ear. "Let me take you home tonight."

She bit her lip, looking uneasy. "You mean to your place?"

"We can go to yours." She'd be more comfortable there, and he wouldn't have to admit he was an officer yet. There'd be no getting away from it if he took her on base.

Ramona's dark gaze looked him up and down, assessing. Then she nodded, as if she'd come to a decision. "Alright." Then she straightened up and pulled out her order pad. "Did you want food or just a beer?"

"I better carb load. I'm going to need my energy." He waggled his brows as he placed an order for a burger and cheese fries. She smirked.

"Looking forward to it, Navy boy."

The Rusty Nail was soon packed. Ramona was rushed off her feet. But she came over to refill his beer and flirt with him. She tended to flirt with most customers—such was business—but he noticed she leaned in further and smiled wider when she was flirting with him.

He'd still tip her well.

After a few beers, he asked her to bring him a Coke. He needed the caffeine to make sure he could stay awake all night.

Jon tensed in his booth late in the night as the crowd got rowdy, and the servers ran around like chickens with their heads cut off. The Orioles game had gone into extra innings, and apparently patrons here were serious about their baseball. And betting on it.

Ramona, in her sexy-as-fuck heels, walked around the corner as one guy knocked a drink on the floor while waving his hands around. It smashed right in front of her just as her heel came down on the hardwood. He watched her leg slide forward, her center of gravity shifting unexpectedly. The realization of what was happening crossed her face as her tray flew backward and her other ankle twisted in her heel as her knee buckled under her. Then she was going down, down, down, and before Jon realized what he was doing, he was running from the booth in the back toward her.

"Mona!"

She hit the floor in a shower of alcohol and glass, and the loud roar in the bar cut off. The total silence should have been jarring, but Jon was only paying attention to one thing.

"Ramona!" Jon skid to a halt, cursing himself for not being fast enough to catch her.

"I'm okay... I think?" She blinked up at him.

"Here, let me help you." He reached out a hand, letting her use him to lift herself to her feet. She stumbled immediately.

"My ankle..."

"We gotta get you out of those shoes."

She shook her head. "It's part of the dress code."

Well, that was bullshit. He wanted to give the owner a piece of his mind, but she was more important. The bartender arrived with a broom and dustpan to sweep up the mess.

"Shit, I'm covered in glass and whiskey," she whined.

"Go home, Ramona. I'll tell Ray what happened," said the older, grizzled bartender.

Ramona looked at him, then at the mess, and then herself. "Okay. Let me just go punch out."

"Can I drive you, Mona?" Jon held onto her as she picked her way through the disaster on the floor.

"That's probably a good idea. It hurts putting weight on it." He helped her to the hallway where the kitchens were. "I'll lean on the wall from here, Sailor. You can't come back here."

"I'll go close my tab and wait here for you."

Leroy, the bartender, reluctantly took his money, saying he ought to make the idiot that caused the wipeout pay for it instead, but Jon didn't want to get Ramona in trouble. Once that was done, he waited not so patiently at the entrance to the back of the bar for Ramona to appear. Naturally, it took twice as long as normal, and his protective instincts were firing on all thrusters. He fought the urge to go back there and get eyes on her again.

When she emerged, still leaning on the wall, he held out his arm gallantly. "My lady, your chariot awaits." She huffed, like she didn't want to laugh but couldn't help it.

"Goofball." Ramona took his arm anyway, the conversations starting to pick back up as the bar recovered from the incident as they made their way to the front door. Once the solid wood door shut closed behind them, and he knew he wouldn't embarrass her, Jon lifted her into his arms bridal style.

"Jon! What are you doing?"

"What I wanted to do inside, but I didn't think you'd appreciate." He marched toward his Dodge Ram, the truck unlocking as he got close with the key fob in his pocket. "Open the door for me, sweetheart." She pulled the handle, and he backed them up, and then slid her inside. "Do you need anything from your car?"

"I have flats in there." She dug around in her purse and handed him the key. "They're in the front passenger side on the floor."

"Yes, ma'am." He gave her a salute and closed the door to the truck.

Jon found the shoes easily and locked her car up tight, then hustled back to his truck. "Will they care if you leave your car?"

She shrugged. "I trust Leroy to let Ray know what happened. If there's a problem, I can come get it tomorrow."

"I guess patrons do it all the time, huh?"

"Not that often, but often enough." She gnawed on her thumbnail. "They do have security cameras."

"Good." He handed her the shoes and clicked his seatbelt into place. Hers was already done, and she bent over to pull her feet out of her heels and slip the comfortable shoes on instead.

"I hope it's not sprained. I don't want to miss more work."

"Let's get it iced anyway, just in case."

She chuckled as she placed the heels on his truck floor. "Honestly, my knee is probably going to be the problem."

"Yeah, that didn't look good."

"I bet I'll feel like one big bruise tomorrow," she sighed as she leaned against the window. "Do you know where you're going?"

"Nope!" He pulled the truck over and took out his phone. Opening his maps app, he handed it to her. "Put your address in, sweetheart."

It didn't take long for them to arrive at her apartment building in the same shitty neighborhood as the dive bar. He didn't want to judge her living space harshly out loud, but it wasn't in great shape.

And of course, she had a third-floor walk-up.

She didn't need his help as much now that she had her flats on, but he stayed close and went at her pace. It soothed his instincts. Jon rubbed a hand over his chest. Ramona could have been seriously hurt tonight. And what if he hadn't been there? How would she have gotten home?

Something about Ramona made him feel the need to protect her, to discover all her secrets. She wasn't forthcoming about a lot of her life, preferring instead to talk about him. But Jon felt she just needed to trust him. And he wanted to learn all about her. To earn her trust.

This was supposed to be a silly bar fling. But it had turned into so much more. Jon wasn't worried. He knew in time she'd come to trust him. He was a good guy. And he had all the time in the world.

He pushed those thoughts from his mind as she unlocked her door. It opened right into a living room, with a small kitchen against the back wall. A hallway that probably led to her bedroom and bathroom extended back into the space.

"Home sweet home." She dropped her keys in a bowl on the entry table and kicked off her shoes. Jon followed suit and set his next to hers.

"Cozy."

"Not much to it, but it's mine." She marched back toward the fridge. "Can I get you a drink?"

"That's my line. You should be elevating that ankle." He double checked that the door was locked and headed toward her.

Shrugging, Ramona pulled out two bottles of water. "I feel much better. I'm just going to take a couple Advil and see how I feel tomorrow."

He tilted his head and watched her move again. "You do seem to be walking better."

"Yeah. I think I just couldn't do those heels anymore after that." She handed him a bottle and sat down on her couch. Well, it was probably a loveseat, but given the small space he wasn't going to split hairs. When she patted the cushion next to her, he kneeled in front of her.

"Jon?"

"Let me just look at your ankles." He lifted her feet into his lap, pushing the legs of her jeans up. They didn't look swollen. Gently, he squeezed them. "How's that feel?"

"Sore, but not too bad."

He kept her feet where they were and rubbed light, slow patterns on them. "Probably not sprained then. But you should definitely stay off your feet for the night."

She groaned. "Damn, that feels good."

He grinned, but didn't massage them any harder, in case he hurt her.

"You should hydrate."

Jon blinked at her. "Beg pardon?"

Her sultry grin made his cock perk up. "You're going to need to stay hydrated."

He chuckled. "Oh really, sweetheart?" Opening the bottle, Jon chugged half of it down. "What did you have in mind?"

She drew her foot along his leg, up from his knee to his groin. "What better way to elevate my ankle?"

Jon jumped to his feet and lifted her into his arms again. "Where's your bedroom? I'll make sure you elevate it all night."

Chapter 3

WARM LIPS NIBBLED AT the edge of Violet's consciousness, tickling her back from dreamland. The early dawn light splayed across her eyelids through a crack in her curtains. She fought not to smile as Jon's kisses trailed down her naked shoulder.

"I know you're awake, baby. How 'bout one more for the road?"

She grunted, pretending to still be asleep.

"Guess I'll have to convince you, then." Strong arms turned her onto her back as the sheets rustled over her. Wet heat traced around first one nipple, then the other, flicking them each in turn.

A familiar ache started up between her thighs. She couldn't help but press them together, attempting to stave it off and keep up the ruse.

That's when he pulled one nipple into his mouth and sucked.

She jolted at the sudden change and stared up at eyes the color of forest moss. "I knew you weren't sleeping," he greeted her with a cocky grin.

To be fair, that cockiness was well-deserved.

She cleared her throat of sleep as his hands and mouth drove her fully awake, and her grunts turned into moans. He slipped two thick fingers into her sheath, fucking her on his hand.

"You're so ready for me."

"Mm-hmm," she agreed as she reached over to her nightstand and grabbed a condom. He took it from her and slid it on his cock, thick and red with arousal.

Gazing up at her muscled Adonis, she wondered at how she'd been lucky enough to catch his eye while working at that shitty bar two months ago. A clean-cut Navy man, with tan skin and an impeccable smile. He could have had anyone there. Yet he picked her.

Sliding into her pussy, he threw his head back and groaned. "Ramona... God, you feel so good, baby."

What she wouldn't give to hear her real name fall from his lips. It was on the tip of her tongue to tell him her actual name, and who she really was. But she couldn't. "Fuck me, Jon." She lifted her hips onto his dick, needing that friction.

"As you wish." Then he gripped her hips and thrust hard, slowly gaining speed until the cheap bed frame smacked against the wall. When he angled his hips just so, it hit right against her G-spot, something no one else had ever found. Was it any wonder she'd kept him around when she was supposed to be invisible?

"Yes, yes, yes!" Stars exploded across her vision as her walls spasmed around him.

Before she'd finished coming down from the afterglow, Jon pulled himself out of her and flipped her over onto her hands and knees with a sharp slap to her ass cheek. She groaned, the heat between her legs roaring back to an inferno.

"You're going to feel me for days, Mona. Tell me no one else fucks you like I do." God, she loved it when Jon let out his inner alpha on her. He wrapped her long hair around his fist and fucked her slow and hard as her back bent toward him.

"No one else fucks me, period, Sailor."

Her pussy wept at his growled response. "That's what I like to hear."

One orgasm bled into the next as he pounded her into next week. Her neighbors had to hate her guts, as she screamed one final time, finally pulling him over the edge with her.

Jon released her hair and fell over her, catching himself on his forearms to hover above her while he caught his breath. Sweat dripped from his forehead and chin that she longed to lick up.

No. Bad Violet. You need to remain detached.

But she knew that ship had sailed weeks ago. Looking up into his eyes, she could see emotions she wasn't ready to deal with. That she *couldn't* deal with. Because she was lying to him. So, preventing him from saying something that would force her to break his heart to his face, she spoke before he could.

"You report back to base today, right?"

"Yeah," he grunted, pulling himself off her with reluctance. "Shower?"

"No way, José. You'll be late if we shower together."

He grinned. "You're not wrong."

Groaning, Violet let him help her sit up, then smacked his tight ass. "Get going, Navy boy. I'll make coffee."

"You're a goddess, Mona."

No, she was a liar. But she couldn't tell him that, so she sent him off with a kiss, locking up behind him.

VIOLET WATCHED THROUGH ANOTHER video, her eyes bleary. After the first round of film hadn't produced any evidence, she'd moved the cameras to the loading dock out the back to see if that produced anything. One camera went on a tree on the edge of the alley, and she'd attached the other to the door.

Speeding ahead to the time when the bar was busiest, she paused on a frame. "Bingo," she murmured to herself. There on the screen was Ray, the manager, passing bags of white powder that could only be drugs to a young man who was handing him a wad of cash. She took a screenshot, then kept watching. It looked like he was supplying the dealers around town, as well as some users. She could tell the difference based on the size of the bags he sold and whether they looked high.

Her data stretched on. Every week, like clockwork, the same buyers showed up over and over.

After copious amounts of coffee, the article was ready to go to her editor. She'd crop the image so no one could see their faces. And while InVestigate couldn't print the full photos without permission, she could definitely have Wanda pass them on to law enforcement once her article went live.

A few clicks of the mouse and Violet's article was done. Now she had to extract herself from the Rusty Nail. And that meant leaving Jon.

Violet rubbed her hand over her chest as it tightened. He was so sweet, and she'd been holding herself back. Lying to him about everything. He thought she'd dropped out of high school when her mama died. That she didn't have any family. Man, had that backfired. He'd tried to convince her to come to his parents' house for their Fourth of July picnic. Thankfully, she'd had to work at the bar that night.

She was supposed to be invisible, forgettable. But Jon saw her. Not the real her, despite his best attempts to get her to open up. But their encounters had been transitioning to more emotional despite her best efforts to keep their relationship purely grounded in the physical.

Which, her reporter's training told her, meant she'd been compromised. Never in her career had she allowed this to happen. What was it about Jonathon that blew her defenses out of the water?

Well, he is *basically a sex god.*

What if Wanda found out? The veteran editor at InVestigate had taken a chance on her a year ago and she wasn't about to lose her dream job because she was thinking with her pussy. There might not be a policy against it specifically, but it was bad form and she knew it.

One of the last things her mom said to her was *"Don't give up your dreams for anyone."* Violet had sworn that to her on her deathbed, along with her brother. Getting caught up with Jon was risking that, big time.

With that, her laptop pinged with a reply to her email. It was Wanda.

Great job, kid! We'll get them shut down for sure.

After Wanda was through with it, the article would print in the next issue of the magazine. Meanwhile, Violet kept up working as Ramona and waiting, watching. Jon kept coming over and banging her brains out. She could have told him the truth now, but if he accidentally blew her cover at the bar, Ray would find out. Guys like that didn't take kindly to snitches. And Violet feared what telling Jon the truth would do to their relationship.

She *should* come clean, she knew. But she didn't want to give him up. And finding out she'd lied the whole time would only drive him away.

No, better to disappear. Her mentor in college would have told her as much. In fact, Carol would have reamed her out for going to the diner with him in the first place.

She could see Carol at the front of the lecture hall, discussing the rules of undercover investigations. Rule number one had been "Be forgettable."

"Your job, when you are undercover, is to blend into the woodwork. Be one with the wallpaper."

Yeah, Violet had blown that all out of the water the minute she flirted back. She dragged out the job, unwilling to give him up right away.

She'd told Wanda she was taking time before her next story. In reality, she was trying to get the courage to come clean to Jon, to figure out a way she could keep seeing him from Virginia. But she ran out of time.

Two days after the issue went live, three weeks after she'd sent her article to Wanda, Violet drove up to the Rusty Nail and squealed internally in excitement. Police cars covered the street, red and blue lights flashing. Detectives and uniformed officers swarmed around the building. Violet slipped her heels on as if she didn't know what was coming. She had one last act to put on.

Chloe stood off to the side of the door, talking to a police officer.

"No, sir, I don't know anything about that. I'm just a waitress here."

"Alright, miss, you're free to go."

The bewildered woman looked at Violet and raced over. How she managed that in her three-inch stilettos without wiping out, Violet wasn't sure.

"Ramona! Oh my God, you'll never believe it!"

"What's going on?"

She bit her plush lower lip as she twisted one of her black curls around her finger. "Ray's been arrested. The owner came down and shut us down for the night."

"Arrested? Shut down?"

Chloe nodded. "I don't know what I'm going to do, my rent's due. I need the money."

"Why did they arrest Ray?"

"I overheard the cops say he's been selling drugs through the back. Right under the owner's nose. They have to close up until the police finish the investigation." She crossed her arms over her ample chest. "Who knows if we'll ever reopen?"

"Seriously?" Ramona feigned shock. "This sucks."

"Guess I better find another job. And get back to the apartment so I don't have to pay the babysitter." Chloe looked at her phone. "Better look up when the next bus gets here."

"My car's here. I'll drive you."

"Thanks, chica. You're the best."

As they pulled out of the parking lot, the yellow and black crime scene tape crossed the doors of the Rusty Nail Saloon. Violet's chest swelled with pride. She'd done that. She'd made it impossible for the authorities to look the other way and she'd taken hundreds of pounds of drugs off the streets. A grieving mother could rest easy knowing that no one else would get drugs here.

Knowing she was following in her idol Nellie's footsteps gave her more satisfaction than she'd thought possible.

Which meant it was time to go.

After dropping Chloe off at her building, Violet headed back to her tiny apartment for the last time. Everything fit into her beater car that she had bought specifically for this assignment. She dropped her key off with the super, making up a story about a sick aunt and that she had to move. Her lease was month-to-month, so they wouldn't come after her.

It wasn't until she got into her car that the image of Jon's face as they made love the night before crossed her mind, and the tears started to flow. Wiping her face with a napkin from the glove box, she put on her road trip playlist and hightailed it out of Annapolis. As much as it hurt, she wanted to get back to her real life by lunch. While Violet may have lost her heart, she was holding onto her career with both hands. She had so many more stories to write.

Jon whistled as he left the florist shop downtown and hopped into his red Dodge Ram. Laying the bouquet of bright red roses on the passenger seat, he sped off toward Ramona's neighborhood. He'd fallen for the dark-haired spitfire over these last two months and couldn't think of anything else except making it official.

While he hadn't donned his dress whites, he *was* wearing a suit when he rolled up to her building. He didn't tell her he was coming back tonight, wanting to surprise her by officially asking her to be his girl.

He'd never gotten serious with someone before, having been the one to break the news to Roger that his high school sweetheart was cheating on him while he was in basic training years ago. It had soured his trust of women, and he never could let anyone that close. Not until Ramona.

His heart pounded in anticipation as he took the stairs two at a time, unable to wipe the excited smile from his face. The thugs hanging around the corner probably looked at him funny, but he didn't care.

When he arrived at apartment 3C, he knocked briskly at the hollow wooden door. Then waited.

And waited.

And waited some more.

He knocked again.

Nothing.

His brow furrowed as he slipped the flowers to his other hand so he could reach in and pull out his cell phone. When he dialed her number, he got something he wasn't expecting at all.

"*The number you have dialed is not in service.*"

What the hell?

"She's gone, sonny." An old woman in a babushka called from across the hall. "I watched her leave this afternoon."

"But... that's... I was here this morning!" He looked at the elderly lady in bewilderment. "I don't understand."

She shrugged her bony shoulders. "If you don't believe me, ask the super." Then she turned and shuffled back into her apartment, shutting the door.

Determination filled him. He'd do that. While he descended the stairs to the manager's apartment, slower this time, he wondered if Ramona had money troubles. Waitresses didn't make a lot of money, especially in shitty dive bars like The Rusty Nail.

He'd have helped her if she needed it! Why wouldn't she come to him? Didn't she trust him?

Jon knocked a bit too firmly on the door marked with an S. A gruff older man with a cigar hanging out of his mouth opened it. "What do you want?"

"Ramona in 3C. She's not answering her door."

"Not here. Moved out this morning."

"Do you know where she went? Did she leave a forwarding address?"

"Nope. Now if that's all, my show's coming on." He shut his door on Jon before he could say a word.

Trudging back to his truck, Jon stared at the flowers in his hand. She'd disappeared. No note, no text message, nothing.

He had to find her.

Before he realized where he was going, Jon found himself on the way to the Rusty Nail. All he had to do was pull into the parking lot to realize this was another dead end. Yellow crime scene tape blocked the door, and a piece of paper taped to the front read "Closed" in a scribbled hand, as if whoever wrote it had been in a rush.

He pulled out his cell phone and stared. Then he dialed Ramona again. The automated voice told him her number was not in service once more.

She was gone.

Suddenly he was fifteen years old again, scraping at the snow lining old Mr. Smith's driveway. It was hard work but it helped him build stamina for the Academy. He'd had to pass a physical when he submitted his application.

Across the street, a door opened and slammed shut. Voices carried across the street. He looked up when he recognized Lacey, his brother's girlfriend's voice.

"I'll see you next week, right, baby?"

"You know it. These study sessions are so … insightful."

The guy his brother's age that lived in that house then grabbed Lacey and kissed her. What the hell? He nearly dropped the shovel to go over there and punch the guy's lights out. Wait a sec… she wasn't pushing him away. In fact, she was holding his shoulders and kissing him back. Pretty sure tongues were involved and everything.

Jon turned away, sick to his stomach. He'd been there when Roger had picked out a necklace at the jewelry store for her Christmas present. Roger was away at basic training and had no idea Lacey was cheating on him. And he'd never believe Jon.

The weight of Mom's digital camera registered in his coat pocket. He'd forgotten he'd borrowed it for a school project. Without thinking about it, he ducked under the stoop, leaning the shovel against the wall. His camera was out and snapping a photo in no time. Roger graduated in two weeks, and the whole family was going down for it. As Lacey got into her car and pulled away, Jon closed his eyes. He was going to break his brother's heart when he saw him again.

Fuck this. Jon didn't need a girlfriend. He needed a fifth of whiskey. With a squeal of his tires, he turned his truck around to head home.

PART II

Chapter 4

Present Day

Violet rubbed a hand over her eyes, the letters on the screen starting to blur together. She'd been sifting through public records for days it seemed, not finding anything on her new quarry.

This company was a ghost town. Which only raised her hackles further.

Flipping back to the anonymous tip sent to the magazine's contact form, she re-read the message, yet she could nearly recite it from memory at this point.

Something weird is going on at Nautical Transit. I never see any boats coming in or going out. We rarely see any employees even though they're headquartered in my small town. A warehouse that big could employ half the town, but no one knows anyone that works there. Or won't admit that they do. It's very strange, and I'd love for one of your writers to look into it. I'm worried something shady is happening here.

Searching for NT's shareholders had only turned up more corporations. Which only gave her more questions.

She needed to find some former or current employees that might be willing to talk to her. So, she opened LinkedUp, a social media site for professionals and corporations, and did a search.

Nothing. No social media presence whatsoever, and the website her internet search pulled up looked like it had been designed for a student portfolio in 2004 and then abandoned.

Violet laid her head in her hands, already feeling the headache building behind her eyes. Who the hell didn't have a social media account in this day and age?

Using satellite imaging for the address only got her so far. The drone must have captured a boat entering the warehouse, which extended over the water. The ship had been partially inside the building, so there must be a way inside. After that, it hadn't taken a genius to determine NT only moved their cargo at night. But that left a lot of options open—anything from drugs to guns to whale oil. The former *Twilight* fangirl in her even wondered if it was run by vampires who didn't want to sparkle in the sun. She giggled to herself as she went over her research notes again.

That did it. She needed a break.

She started her electric kettle and rummaged through her tea bag collection. It was too late in the afternoon for caffeine, so she settled on an herbal blend that should help her brainstorm.

Violet woke up the next morning slumped over her desk with a crick in her neck. Her tea was cold and her cell phone alarm was going off. Damn it. She had to go into the office today to give Wanda an update.

She brushed her teeth and showered, then dressed quickly in her trousers and a lilac blouse. Wrapping her hair up in a chignon, she swiped on the barest bit of make-up, poured coffee into a thermal travel cup and grabbed a breakfast biscuit from the open box on her counter. She could eat in traffic.

Gainesville, Virginia was well outside D.C. but the traffic could still be brutal. The office was just on the capital's outer city limits, by one of the last Metro stations. The location made getting to the city and all its political events much easier for the politics division, but Violet wished she could go fully remote and not have to deal with the commute. She only worked from the building when necessary as it was, opting to do most of her writing and research from her condo, but Wanda wanted an in-person meeting to discuss the Nautical Transit article.

She parked her car, leaving her permit sitting on the dashboard, and then lifted her laptop bag out of the passenger side and made her way toward the office. Flashing her badge at the door let her inside, where she waved to the security guard and took the elevator to the second floor. Her cubicle was just as she'd left it, the photo of her with her mom and brother at his high school graduation sitting in its frame. Before Mom got sick. Next to that was a picture of her and her brother's drag persona, a more recent addition from her latest trip to New York where he lived.

Shaking away the melancholy, she hooked her laptop up to the network and checked her email. The meeting with Wanda was at nine, but she liked to clock in at eight even when she was on site.

Petra, the office gossip, was making her rounds. She stopped by Violet's desk. "Hey Violet, how's it going?"

"It's going well. How about you?" Violet wanted to be polite.

The tall willowy woman grimaced. "Mark said his wife filed for divorce."

"That's a shame." Violet wasn't entirely surprised, though. Mark was one of their best journalists and over the five years she'd worked at InVestigate, one truth was universal—balancing a family with this career was impossible. It was just one reason why she herself remained a single Pringle.

"Yeah, he's upset. Took the day off, obviously. I don't know what's going to happen to his story on the Chinese importer."

Great. Wanda would already be stressed. And she wasn't making any headway on her own story. This was the last thing Violet needed.

But she would never let Petra know she was concerned. "I'm sure we'll be fine. That company isn't going anywhere."

"True. Well, I'll see you around."

"Yup." As soon as she was alone, Violet released a sigh. Her mind wandered to her late-night dates from four years ago with Jon, that sailor she'd met while undercover in Annapolis. She'd gotten too close, nearly blowing her cover with him. But she sometimes wondered what would have happened if she'd told him who she was once the story broke.

He was a gentleman in the streets, and a control freak in the sheets. The way he'd rescued her when she fell at the bar and twisted her ankle indicated an overprotective streak a mile wide, which she'd also gleaned from their conversations about his baby sister. No, that wouldn't have ended well. She'd be in Mark's position sooner or later. That's why she'd disappeared on Jon without a word. Those memories could live in perpetuity, a snow globe on her shelf she could take down on lonely nights when it was just her and her vibrator.

Later, though. Right now, Violet needed to work.

When nine o'clock rolled around, Violet shook the nerves from her hands and locked her computer before heading into Wanda's office. She knocked, then Wanda called out.

"Come in."

Opening the door, Violet slipped into her editor's office. A window along the back wall showed a tiny glimpse of the Washington Monument in the distance along with a deceptively bright blue sky. It was chilly outside, but it appeared to still be fall with the bare trees. Dishonest, really. They were already in winter. Wanda's desk was covered in paperwork and Wanda herself looked frazzled. Her salt and pepper bob looked like she'd been running her hands through it. The older woman gestured at the two guest chairs in front of her mahogany desk. "Sit down and tell me where we're at on the Nautical Transit piece."

Violet sat on the edge of her seat, crossing one leg over the other in an attempt to look poised. "What do you want to know?"

Her boss leaned on her arms as they lay across the desk. "Any idea when we can run it? I need something to replace the Chinese importer article Mark is working on."

Violet swallowed. "I don't know. I'm hitting dead ends everywhere. The shareholders are other corporations. No one admits to working for them. I can't even find a social media presence or internet reviews. NT is a ghost, Wanda."

Wanda groaned and palmed her forehead. "Have you gone and talked to them in person yet?"

Violet shook her head. "That was going to be my next step." It wasn't, but that's not something Wanda needed to know. It just got moved up the timeline.

"Try emailing or calling, first. Best not to surprise anyone if you can help it."

She stopped short of rolling her eyes. "Or that will give them a chance to get rid of the evidence before I get in there."

Wanda shrugged. "Your call, kid. I trust you." She waved her off, and Violet knew she was dismissed. "I don't want to see you again until the article is finished, you hear?"

"But what about—"

"You let me worry about replacing Mark's article. That's what they pay me for. Now what do you need to get this thing done?"

Violet huffed. "I can try calling them. I'll say I work for a different publication and see if they're willing to talk to me about business. But if that doesn't work, I might need a hacker."

Wanda laughed. "Nothing that illegal, okay?"

"Alright." Violet pretended to pout. This was one of their ongoing jokes. They were both women fighting to make it in a man's industry. Violet was willing to get results by any means necessary. But being older, Wanda preferred her people to use the tried-and-true journalistic methods, though she hadn't been upset at the results Violet's under-cover work had gotten them. After all, that article on the Rusty Nail Saloon had won an award four years ago.

"I'll talk to you later, Wanda."

"Good luck, kid."

Jon sat at his parents' dining table, the familiar gold striped wallpaper surrounding him, his parents, his siblings, and their partners. Mom was trying to convince Nadia to do a summer wedding, but since it was January, most places were already booked. Nadia wanted an October wedding; she wanted the fall colors for her backdrop. Poor Caleb looked torn, since Mom and Dad were footing a lot of the bill, but he wanted Nadia happy most of all.

Jon appreciated that about him.

He passed Roger the butter for his mashed potatoes before Roger even asked. While his body was present, his mind kept reminding him of that awful meeting he'd attended last week.

Jon shivered at the memory even though he desperately wanted to forget and lose himself in his family. But his conscience wouldn't let him.

How had he spent so long in the Navy without seeing the blatant misogyny? Had he just ignored it? Had people not shown that side of themselves to him knowing he was super protective of Nadia? Hell, he'd kept her picture in his dorm room and more than one person asked if she was his daughter.

They'd heard his stories and laughed along about sitting on the porch with his brothers and their dad cleaning their guns when a guy came to pick her up for a date. But he'd never thought they'd sweep a rape case under the rug.

Jon read along the meeting agenda as they went through this boring-ass staff meeting. Then he realized Wesson skipped over a bullet point on the list; that wasn't like him. "Sir? What about this 'insubordination issue'? Shouldn't we go over that?"

Wesson huffed. "Everyone here knows about it."

"This is the first I've heard of it." Jon tilted his head. "I'd like to understand."

Abrams rubbed the back of his neck. "All you need to know is it's being dealt with. We had to put it on the agenda for paperwork reasons."

The hairs on the back of Jon's neck rose. Something was off about this. "Then we should discuss it."

"There's nothing to discuss, it's been handled." Wesson scowled at him.

Jon scrubbed a hand over his face. "Will someone tell me what the fuck is going on?"

Abrams sighed. "I had an ensign accuse a petty officer of misconduct."

"What kind of misconduct?" Jon narrowed his eyes at his colleague.

"She claimed he attacked her in the stairwell. There are no cameras there. It's his word against hers. And she refused to go to the infirmary."

Jon's blood turned to ice in his veins. "He raped her?"

"We don't know. But she's been disciplined for the false accusation."

His fist slammed down on the table. "How do you know it's false? Why would she lie about this?"

Wesson waved his hand to dismiss the notion. "Women do it all the time for attention, Hunt. Now, let's move on to—"

"You had a victim come to you and you punished her? What is wrong *with you?"*

"Hunt! If you don't shut the fuck up right now, you're looking at your own insubordination write up, and you have a pension to lose. Now, as I was saying..."

Jon felt his face turning red as the memory played. He'd barely heard anything the rest of the meeting, sitting there fuming and reminding himself that if he threw a punch at Abrams, he was only going to hurt himself. It wouldn't achieve justice for the victim.

He couldn't believe he'd gotten wrapped up in such a disgusting organization.

Jon tried to remember the good the Navy did, but he was failing miserably. And he just wanted out.

If he resigned now, he wouldn't have much of a pension. He needed another job. One where he could trust the people that ran it not to be dicks.

He sipped at his water while Finn talked about the road trip he wanted to take Josie on. He'd missed when they were planning to leave. Then Roger started talking about

Sam and Frankie taking on the cyber security work he'd been approached about.

Roger would never put up with the shit he'd witnessed last week. And the more Roger talked about how many contracts he had to turn away, the stronger an idea formed in Jon's head. Roger needed help. Jon needed a new purpose.

"Having too much work is a good problem to have, Roger." Mom chimed in as she started collecting dishes.

"Yeah, who knew guarding a senator's daughter would get me so much publicity?" Roger shook his head.

"At least my dad was good for something," Jenna sighed.

Jon decided to shoot his shot. "Hey Rog, why don't I come work for you?"

The clanking of dishes stopped as everyone went still. "What about your career?"

Jon leaned back in his chair. Legally, he couldn't discuss what had happened in the meeting, it was classified. But he could tell them what he'd decided. "I'm resigning my commission. It's not what I want anymore."

Roger narrowed his eyes. "We'll talk. Give me the dishes, Mom, Jon and I are going to clean up." Jon took his cue and started gathering up the dirty plates near him and then followed his brother out to the kitchen.

"You boys don't have to do that!"

"No, let them, Mom." Nadia waved at her. Jon chuckled to himself, knowing his baby sister was enjoying this. "They need the practice."

"Practice? Your brothers have been living on their own for a long time."

"You'll never let me live down those dishes in my dorm, will you, Nad?" Jon called out.

"Nope!"

While Roger rinsed, Jon filled the dishwasher. Under the cover of the running sink, they could talk somewhat privately. "Are you sure about resigning, Jon?"

"I'm sure." Roger being former Army had probably seen his own shit, and he wouldn't put it past the former Green Beret to mete out his own justice if Jon blabbed. Which he couldn't do, anyway. But he could give him a hint. "It's not the same. Something happened and I can't stand working with them anymore."

"They do something to you?" Roger stiffened, wiping his hands on the towel. Only four years separated them, but he was ever the protective big brother, ready to hand someone's ass to them on the playground.

"Not to me. You know I'm not allowed to say anything. But I can't do this anymore. It's just been years of ineffectual leadership, and now the incoming administration wants to make a social media personality with no military experience the Secretary of Defense. What happened was just the last straw. And…" he eyed the kitchen door. "It's time to come home."

Roger slapped a hand on his shoulder. "I'd be happy to have you."

Jon grinned. "Thanks, man. I'll get the ball rolling on retirement and then I'm all yours."

"Let me know when you have a start date. I could definitely use the extra man power."

"You're going to need a bigger office."

Roger pinched the bridge of his nose. "I don't like the idea of renting space. What if the jobs dry up?"

Jon waved his finger at him. "You can't think like that. Maybe just a small outbuilding on that property of yours to start. Get a trailer or something so people don't have to be in your personal house."

Roger smacked him with the towel. "Hunt Security is family. And I'm going to keep it that way."

"Quality over quantity. I like it." Jon grinned as he popped a detergent pod into the machine and closed the door. "Think Mom made dessert?"

"Does a bear shit in the woods?"

While Mom served apple crumble, Jon pulled out his phone and started looking for rental properties in the area. Finn living with Mom and Dad had been a disaster, and a mistake Jon wasn't keen to emulate. His younger brother and his girl Josie were still living in Roger's guest room, for some reason. So, he'd need to line up a place of his own before retiring.

Thank God for his brother. Jon couldn't wait to start this next chapter of his life.

Chapter 5

Phone calls went ignored. Violet left half a dozen voicemails before she tracked down an email address and sent a request for an interview with her trumped up spiel. She received a polite but firm dismissal. So, she got a hotel in the nearby city of Roanoke and forwarded the receipt to Wanda.

The email response had been interesting.

Can't get them to pick up?

They can't ignore me if I'm standing there.

Violet was sure Wanda was snickering over her predicament. But this is why she'd given Violet this assignment. She was like a dog with a bone when it came to her stories.

That's why she put on her smartest skirt suit, donned her press pass for the fake publication they all had to use whenever getting information from unwilling sources, and drove down to the Nautical Transit warehouse herself.

She passed through the small town of Eastfield, a slice of Americana with its classic town square. A certain big box store with a blue logo loomed from a hill overlooking the town, and Violet shook her head. Companies like that tended to move in and run small businesses out. No wonder people were looking for answers about potential other jobs.

The parking lot for the warehouse had a handful of cars, not nearly enough to account for a four-story building full of employees. And it was quiet, too quiet. No one shouting orders, no employees leaning against the building for a smoke break. Hell, it was just after lunch and the picnic tables outside were completely empty. Although that could just be because of the cold weather and the wind off the water. Picking up her black leather folio with the legal pad inside, she strutted to the front door on her stiletto heels.

The metal and glass door swung outward, but that's where she stopped. In front of her in the tiny vestibule sat a beefy security guard, who might have been attractive without that mountain man beard and the scowl on his face. Then he rose to his full height. How was he not scraping the ceiling?

"Can I help you?"

"Yes, I'm Violet with the Newport Gazette, I reached out to your manager about the article we're doing on the local businesses."

"Lady, you shouldn't be here."

She didn't like the way he eyed her, but she stayed still. It wouldn't do to let him know he gave her the creeps. Attraction was definitely out the window with that leer on his face.

"I've been trying to reach the person in charge and since they're so busy my boss told me to come down in person to get the profile done." Another lie, but he didn't need to know that. "It'll only take a few minutes."

"No press. Now get out," he growled.

The hair on the back of Violet's neck rose, and she started to step back toward the exit. But she had to give it one last shot. "I can do the interview over the phone. Can I leave my number with you?" She even batted her eyelashes for good measure.

"*OUT!*"

Clearly, she wasn't going to get anywhere with this lug. Violet shoved the door open and stalked off. She opened her car door and threw her folio into the passenger seat with a thunk, then slammed it shut. "Fucking creeper," she said to herself, and backed out of the space and drove back to the town proper.

She'd feel safer with more people around.

Stopping at a small hole in the wall sandwich shop, she stuffed her fake press pass into her purse and decided InVestigate could treat her to lunch as a business expense. Over a chicken wrap and fries, Violet mulled the whole interaction over in her head. They were definitely hiding something big. No one turned down free publicity unless they had something they didn't want brought to light. What Cerberus had done wasn't going to drive her away. Instead, he'd piqued her interest further and only made her more determined to figure out what was going on at Nautical Transit.

Nellie Bly had faked insanity to get into the asylum. How could Violet get inside this warehouse?

"WE'RE GONNA MISS YOU, man." Ben, one of Jon's fellow officers, drunkenly slurred. Jon patted him on the back and wondered how he was planning to get home tonight.

"Yeah, I know, but it's time."

"Take care of yourself."

"You too!"

He sipped at his beer, only his second of the night, gazing around at the officer's club that his commander had reserved entirely for this retirement party. He'd served with these men, but not in the way that Roger and Sam had served together. There was always an odd disconnect between him and the others, being in charge of different groups. Most of the people he'd gone to the Academy with had ended up leaving the area, only a small portion making it through the grueling process, and more moving on to other jobs within the Navy. He was a rarity that had stayed in the area for his whole career.

Still, despite living here since he was seventeen, Annapolis wasn't home.

That's why he'd spent so much time at the Rusty Nail when it was still open. There, he wasn't Lieutenant Hunt; he was just Jon, an average Joe who told women he was in the Navy when they asked what he did. He could go back to their homes and get his release without worrying about an ethics inquiry in the morning.

He'd gone back looking for Ramona the night after she disappeared, hoping to see her and hopefully get an explanation. But the bar had still been closed. Eventually, he found out they wouldn't be reopening. He'd heard on the news that the manager had been running drugs through the back and got caught. Fucking scumbag. Years later, someone had bought it and turned it into a hipster gastro pub. The food was good, but no one there knew what had happened to Ramona. It had been a long shot to even try, but he'd been lonely one night and nobody had caught his eye at his new haunt.

And these guys had never been his friends. That had been made clear two months ago in that God-awful meeting. The one that had made him want to resign his commission and hang up his uniform. He'd had to look these men in the eyes and wonder which of them were guilty of the same crime they'd covered up. Jon was ashamed to be a part of this organization anymore.

"Cake!" The shout pulled him back to the present as a server wheeled out a cart with a giant sheet cake sitting on top. Covered in balloons made of frosting, it read, "Best wishes, Lieutenant Hunt."

His commander waved him over. "Come on, Jon, you do the honors." He approached the side table as the servers lifted the cake onto a side table. Commander Daughtry found a knife and pressed into his palm.

"What, you mean I gotta *share*?" Jon's joke made the whole room laugh as he thanked the server for the plates she handed him from the cart.

Cutting such a huge cake was no joke. When his hand started to cramp, someone else took over cutting pieces of cake. He made sure he got a corner piece, since the icing was the best part.

When the party was finally over and Jon could get away, he slid into his red Dodge Ram and closed his eyes. He didn't think he'd shaken this many hands or had his back slapped so much ... ever. Funny how people made you feel welcome the moment you decided to leave.

He'd expected his resignation to take longer to process, but the Navy had approved it quickly. Had Wesson had a hand in that? It didn't matter anymore. The movers were coming in the morning to transport everything to his new house in Baltimore.

He hadn't been this excited about anything in a long time.

Jon rolled up to his house for the last time. Once he had his employment settled for a while, he'd look into buying his own place, but he didn't like the idea of house hunting from Annapolis. He'd packed all his knickknacks away, his photos as well. Around his living room sat boxes labeled "LARP", "Dungeons and Dragons", "Kitchen", and "Books". Clothing was in a separate box. He'd get the movers to help him load his truck; he only needed them for the furniture, after all. Nothing was left but a bland beige box.

He programmed his coffee pot, one of the last things to get put away, and set his alarm for morning. But even after a shower, he lay in bed thinking about his time in Annapolis. And time he'd spent at the Rusty Nail.

A tall, dark-eyed beauty, long raven hair over one shoulder showing off the strappy back of her skin-tight tank top. Her painted-on skinny jeans held a peach that would fit perfectly in his hands.

And it had. So many times. For a guy who didn't do relationships, their fling had been the closest thing he'd gotten to one.

"Hello, there," that sultry voice greeted him as she turned around. He caught a glimpse of her perfectly mouth-sized breasts encased in that lucky shirt as she leaned back against the bar. But he kept his eyes on her face.

"Can I buy you a drink?"

Memories of Ramona woke his cock. Ever since she ghosted him, his libido hadn't been the same. It had made life at LARP events interesting. He'd always been down for a decent fuck, and if he took a girl back to his tent, he made sure she had a good time, but that didn't always mean his dick got into the action. He'd actually been missing more events in the last few years than he'd attended, partly because of that, blaming it on work. The last time he'd gone to Armageddon he'd met a pair of women who were just as into each other as they were into him, and it had worked out well, but the threesome hadn't turned into the mind-blowing event he'd thought it would be. It hadn't helped him forget the one that got away.

Why was he still hung up on her after all this time? Jon didn't know. But he'd have to take himself in hand as he remembered all the time he'd spent at her place. They'd christened every surface in that shitty apartment. Memories of bending her over the couch, lifting her and fucking her against that wall ... God, those had been amazing times.

His hand found his cock, and he jerked himself, fast and hard like she always wanted it. He came much faster than he wanted to, like his dick had been waiting for that to do its job. While he cleaned up in the bathroom, he wondered what had happened. Why did she disappear on him? He rubbed at the tightness in his chest that always accompanied the memory of showing up to her apartment and finding her gone. They hadn't done much other than hang out at the Nail and fuck, but he'd fallen for her just the same. Naïve of him, he knew. But finding someone that saw beyond the uniform was rare in his experience.

And in the end, it didn't matter, anyway. She'd disappeared.

It had taken him so long to trust a woman, any woman, after catching his brother's sweetheart cheating on him. And yet, that trust had ended up misplaced anyway. Jon had written off any hope of a relationship for himself, despite the envy that smacked him in the chest every time he was around his siblings and their partners. Women only wanted him for a good time, not a long time.

Jon climbed back into bed and closed his eyes, worn out. Tomorrow was the beginning of the next chapter of his life.

Chapter 6

"THIS ISN'T LIKE YOU, Violet."

Violet leaned against the hotel room wall, her phone at her ear. She could see Wanda's disappointed face in her mind's eye. It put a sour taste in her mouth, but she was trapped in this phone call.

The last thing she wanted to do was disappoint her boss.

"Do you want to take over the China article from Mark?"

What the hell? "What happened to Mark?"

"He's taken a leave of absence. I don't think he's coming back." Wanda sighed. "Another one bites the dust."

Violet chewed on her lip, silently agreeing with Wanda. But Mark had to make his own decisions about his priorities. Anyone could write that article, she knew Mark's research would be sound, and he'd have everything laid out for whoever took it over. But it wasn't what she wanted to write. Something about this Nautical Transit had her hackles raised and at this point she was willing to do anything to get the scoop.

"Give me one more chance. If I can't get inside with this, I'll give up the story."

Wanda paused, and her chair creaked in the background as if she'd sat up straighter. "What are you thinking?"

"I'm applying for a job there."

"Vi, are you sure?" Wanda wasn't a fan of her people going undercover. She always said it was better to obtain their information from safe sources, like emails and interviews. Mainstream techniques were fine and all. Violet could use them as well as the next reporter. But each story was different and Violet liked the acting involved with infiltrating a business. She was the only one who dared do it on the regular, or at least she used to. But Wanda didn't know she'd been compromised four years ago.

"I really don't see a choice, Wanda," Violet flipped back through her notes. "I need to get eyes on the place, especially since they won't talk to me." They had stonewalled her both virtually and in person.

Her longtime editor groaned, and Violet could almost hear the vein thumping in her forehead. "I don't like it, Vi."

"Hey, it worked for the Rusty Nail article. And this could be even bigger."

"Or it could just be a case of a stupid little rich boy's idea of a career. With private companies, we don't know."

Violet spoke before Wanda could launch into her usual lecture about ethics and people's right to privacy. "But that's the thing. Nautical Transit isn't private, not really. They still have investors and they have to answer to stockholders."

"And have you located any of these stockholders?"

Wanda knew the answer just as Violet did. No, she had not. The investors listed were all corporate entities, at least as far as she'd been able to ascertain.

"The paper trail leads nowhere. We've monitored traffic on their website and their customer parking lot, and there's no one even searching for them. Something is fishy and I know you smell it, too."

Wanda sighed, and Violet knew she had her cornered. "Alright, but be careful, okay? I want regular updates. Get in, get your information, and get the fuck out of there."

"Of course." Violet's heart pounded. She always got the best scoops when she followed her idol's example. Her most successful stories all originated this way.

"If you miss more than one check-in, I'm calling for help."

She gulped. Wanda hadn't always agreed with her more unorthodox methods, but hadn't been able to argue with the results. And since most businesses she investigated usually had ex-employees willing to talk, she hadn't had to utilize those methods in years. Not since the Rusty Nail.

And *that* article had won her awards! She was itching for another one and something told her this was going to be huge.

After she finished her call with Wanda, she hit send on the message she'd had ready to go to the email listed for Nautical Transit, attention their HR department. Within minutes, even though it was after eight o'clock on a Wednesday night, she had a refusal for the fake resume she'd set up.

Ms. Ward,

I regret to inform you that there are no positions open for a lady of your training at NT. Currently, only warehouse positions are open and too much lifting is required. We will be in touch if our needs change.

> *Thank you,*
>
> *HR*

They didn't even give her a name! It was too short to be a form letter. And gender discrimination was illegal, though good luck proving it. If she'd actually been interested in a job, Violet would have taken it up with the proper authorities. And this would certainly find its way into her finished piece. They were basically saying, "Women need not apply." But she didn't actually want to work for them, so she needed a new plan.

Think, Violet, think! What would Nellie do?

She paced around her hotel room in Roanoke. NT was located along the coast a couple of hours south. She'd need a home base near there, so she'd better look up cheap studio apartments she could rent on her base pay at InVestigate.

But all this research was for nothing if she couldn't get inside because of her gender.

What would Nellie do? How would she get around this block?

Her eyes landed on a photo of her and her brother, Callum, at the drag show back in New York where he'd been Emcee. They stood next to a drag king whose name she didn't remember. But that sparked a kernel of an idea in her and she snapped her fingers. Of course!

First, to see if it worked.

She carefully crafted a new resume with a different name and more compelling work history. After creating an email for her new persona, she filled out the application a second time. This resume got a very different response.

We'd love to discuss our warehouse opening with you on Monday. Which of these times works best for you?

Now she had until Monday to figure out her disguise. Her next phone call was to her brother. He picked up on the first ring.

"Hey sissy, can I call you back?"

"It's important, Cal." She pinched the bridge of her nose. "Are you at a show?"

"It's just wrapping up. Seriously, I'll call in ten minutes."

"Okay, fine." She hung up, then started looking online for salons nearby that would cater to her unique need. Fifteen minutes later, Cal called back.

"Vivi, what's up?"

"I need some advice. I'm in Roanoke getting ready to go undercover but I have to look like a guy."

She could almost hear him blinking at her with those long false lashes he wore as Anita Dik, his drag persona.

"Come again?"

"Ew, you're my brother."

"Sorry, automatic response." He paused and she could hear him calling out to the dressing room, "Any of you bitches from Virginia?" Then he came back on the line. "I'm not sure what you're asking for help with."

"I was thinking of finding a queer-friendly barber or hair salon so they don't ask too many questions. And I should probably disguise my face somehow."

"Yeah, you don't have a chin that screams 'masculine', which is normally a good thing." He sighed. "A quick Google search should help you with the barber. I might cry when you cut off all that gorgeous hair. But why do you need to go undercover as a dude?"

"Because these idiots won't talk to me or accept my application for employment as a woman. And there's something going on here, Cal. I know it." Callum was familiar with her gut instinct, despite it failing her when their mom got sick.

Callum hummed into the phone. "Hang on, let me get Lex."

Lex Luwhore was one of the drag kings Anita performed with. Their androgynous voice came over the line next. "Hey Vivi, what's going on?"

"Long story short, I need to go undercover as a guy. Any tips?"

"I can send some make up tips through Anita's phone, but if you're going to be working closely with people there you probably want to get fake facial hair. Check a theater store."

"Ooh, thanks, Lex! Can you put Anita back on?"

"Sure thing, honey. Nita, bitch! Your phone."

Callum/Anita came back to her phone. "Did they help? I was taking my lashes off."

"Yes, thanks so much. Listen, I may not be in contact for a while. I'll have to switch to a burner phone."

Her brother's voice got deadly serious. "Be safe, Sis, okay? Anyone willing to discriminate is bad news."

"I will."

The next day, she headed out to the tiny theater supply store in Roanoke. They had everything she needed, and since she'd be a couple of hours away, she loaded up on extra wig glue. Then she made her way to a small hair salon she'd found online, a Pride flag in the window. A tall person in full drag stood behind the counter.

The bell on the door pinged as she shut it behind her. "Can I help you?"

"Hi. I need a haircut. Do you take walk-ins?"

"We do. You'll have to wait."

"That's fine. I have time." She gave her name at the desk, then took a seat. Violet realized she would have to do some shopping as well, find a thrift store to get her disguise right. A warehouse job interview wouldn't require a full suit, right?

She fell down a rabbit hole online trying to figure out what her style as Victor would be. The name was her nod to the Broadway musical, *Victor/Victoria*, about a woman masquerading as a man. Callum had dragged her to see it in New York during the revival, and despite not being a theater person, she'd thought it was hilarious. He'd sent her the 1982 film for her birthday.

Would she need a binder? Probably not. She barely needed a bra most days. As a member of the Itty-Bitty Titty Committee, Violet never had an issue with the backless dresses she often wore to parties for her magazine.

After deciding to keep it simple with baggy tees and hoodies, she heard her name called. Looking up, she saw a tall gentleman in a bright pink waistcoat waving her over. His long platinum blonde hair was tied back, and his eyeliner was sharp enough to cut someone.

She wished she could get makeup lessons from this guy.

He draped the cape around her shoulders and pulled her hair out. "I'm Freddy. So, what are we doing today?"

Violet closed her eyes with a grimace. "I need to look like a guy." Freddy tilted his head at her. She rushed to explain. "It's a temporary thing, for a job."

"Oh, are you in a play? Why wouldn't you just wear a wig?"

"It, uh… it didn't fit." She lied easily enough. "It's just hair, it'll grow back."

"Hmmm." Freddy drew his long, painted fingers through her dark locks as she watched in the mirror. "How old is your character?"

"He's in his twenties."

"Modern times?"

She nodded.

"Okay. I'll cut it so when it grows out it'll be more like a pixie cut, but the in between process is going to be brutal."

"I know. This means a lot to me."

"Well, don't let anyone say you're not dedicated." He fluffed her hair out, then drew his scissors. "As long as you're sure."

"I'm sure."

With every snip of his shears, more and more hair fell away. When it came time to sculpt the style around her face, he turned her chair around to face away from the mirror. He cleaned up the back with an electric shaver, then spun her back around. "What do you think?"

Holy. Shit. Violet didn't even recognize herself. She looked like she could be in a boy band. Her hair parted neatly down the middle, the longest pieces on top hanging on either side of her forehead. She'd never had hair shorter than her chin, so this was very different.

"It's perfect." Her own mother wouldn't know her on the street.

She was going to do her idol Nellie proud.

THE GIANT RED BRICK warehouse took up two city blocks in the small town of [Redacted] and was the entirety of its waterfront center. Surprising, when the tourism trade should be booming in a town on the water.

Violet's article practically wrote itself. She'd started it shortly after her interview at Nautical Transit. And now, she was working there. Under false pretenses, sure, and she'd be in legal trouble if they discovered she'd lied on the application. But that's why the paychecks were going to a dummy account in case she got caught. She didn't need the pittance they were paying, anyway. If everything at NT turned out to be above board, she'd quit quietly and donate what they'd paid her to charity. And if things were what she thought they were, the money would still go to charity, it just would be to an organization that would help the victims of whatever the hell Nautical Transit was doing.

But out of all the jobs she'd done in her life, this had to be the most boring.

It was simple, really. But it left her with too much time to think and isolated her entirely in Norm's office. The freak was absolutely paranoid about his computer files. Her current assignment was to copy every file from his desktop computer to a five-terabyte hard drive.

Every. God. Damn. File.

Half of them had nonsense names. The other half were named like her grandmother's cookbook. Why the hell did he need these?

At least there were a few windows in the yellow cinder block walls.

"Hey, Victor. How many more files do you have left in that folder?" Norm, the big boss at NT, asked from his perch on the file cabinet. His paunchy belly gave him the unassuming air of a mediocre white man who peaked in high school. The gray combover showed his age. How could he have so many digitized files yet still use a locking file cabinet? Fucking boomer.

"There's a lot here, Norm," she struggled to keep the annoyance out of her tone, and fought the urge to scratch at her fake beard. The hairs under her nose were going to make her sneeze again. How was she supposed to eavesdrop on anything with the two of them stuck in his office?

Norm looked at his watch. "I'm going to grab a sandwich. Can I bring you something back?"

Her stomach chose that moment to growl, not giving her a choice. "Sure."

Finally, she was alone. He really didn't need to stand guard over her while she copied files from one place to another, then deleted them from the original computer. This was busy work and she knew it.

He didn't trust her yet.

But now she was alone with his entire computer for a few glorious minutes. She had to act fast before he came back. What was the deal with Nautical Transit?

Double-clicking on a file marked "Main Course," which was so original Violet wanted to roll her eyes, she scanned what turned out to be a list of names.

Naturally, he was using red herrings as file names. Her journalist senses started tingling like they had when she first tried to get into the building. The hairs on the back of her neck stood straight up. Despite her black hoodie, she shivered.

She knew these names. A lot of them, anyway. Last year she'd been assigned a story that she hadn't been able to finish, which did happen occasionally, even to the best of them. Wanda had asked her to look into an alleged theft ring that targeted museums with valuable gems on display and resold the stolen goods, which were usually on loan from wealthy patrons. The gems would disappear, then reappear at an auction house with different names and different settings. She'd managed to get her hands on the list of the buyers from the auction house and she recognized a good dozen or so. None of these people had ever indicated they knew they'd bought stolen goods, but between the secretive nature of the museums and the patrons who loaned out their collections, she hadn't been able to make any headway. Apparently, embarrassment was enough of a deterrent to keep that community from talking.

It was stupid, really. Bad enough the museums had to deal with higher insurance rates, but they basically flat out refused to participate in the investigation and wanted their names kept out of any and all publications. She'd been professionally hamstringed.

Was Nautical Transit involved in shipping the gems? She still hadn't made it to the warehouse floor. But as Norm's footsteps echoed down the hall, she closed the file and made a mental note to come back to this lead later.

SHE STRUTTED DOWN THE second-floor hallway, hands in her black hoodie pocket. It had been two weeks of working at the warehouse. She did appreciate that this undercover persona got to wear comfortable clothes and sneakers. So far, she'd spent most of her time scanning files into Norm's computer and then immediately moving them to his external hard drive. And then she'd been relegated to standing around and moving boxes of generic supplies. The guys that worked there had stopped eyeing her with quite so much suspicion, which was good. She needed to earn their trust to find out what was going on.

At least she'd quickly figured out why no one ever left. The third and fourth floors were dormitories for the employees. Saving money on the studio apartment she'd planned to rent was great, but she had to sneak up to the roof to make her check ins with Wanda. She was on what Norm had called "probation." He'd confiscated her burner phone. Unbeknownst to him, though, she'd had a backup hidden in her bag. So, the last thing she needed was someone overhearing her conversations with Wanda.

Thus far she hadn't missed a single check-in.

Violet peered around the corner, her ears perked for the boss's footsteps. Her journalist senses were tingling, alerting her that she was almost to the juicy bits of information. Creeping down the hallway, she rubbed at the fake beard. The damn thing itched something fierce, and she didn't have a good excuse for the way it didn't grow. So far, no one had noticed.While her alter-ego was just a grunt working the warehouse, she was determined to discover how a floundering business was still in operation.

Part of the problem is the misogyny, she thought to herself. They wouldn't accept her for a warehouse position as a female, so she'd had to fake a male identity just to get the interview. Nellie Bly would be proud. Wanda would shit a brick if she knew.

Her footsteps slowed as she approached the boss's office. He was on the phone.

"What do you *mean,* you lost one?" Norman's voice didn't sound happy. "How hard is it to move a shipment of merchandise?"

She couldn't hear what the flunky on the other side of the conversation was saying. But by the huffing and puffing coming from Norm's office, it wasn't acceptable.

"Put him on the line." He waited a beat. "How many times do I have to tell you not to damage the merchandise?"

Violet crept closer. She'd been summoned at the end of her shift, but her mama always taught her not to interrupt when someone was on their phone. And she'd discovered as a teen that was the best time to eavesdrop.

"Oh, this one had a mouth on her, did she? It's your fault you lost her. Now find her before she runs her mouth again. We already know the cameras were tapped. You're only lucky the FBI didn't find anything when they went through the safe house. And bring her alive." His voice deepened. "I want to question her myself."

Violet's heart pounded in her chest so loud she was sure it could be heard in the dimly lit hallway. Women? The merchandise was *women?*

Thoughts warred in her head. Leaving this early would mean she didn't have enough for her article, but if she got in any deeper, they'd never let her alter ego go.

Evidence. She needed *evidence.* And she had to call her editor tonight. This was way bigger than either of them had anticipated. She wasn't due for a check-in just yet, but Wanda wouldn't complain.

Her mind made up, she waited until the phone slammed down into its cradle. Then she turned the corner.

"Hey, boss. You wanted to see me?" Thank goodness for her natural contralto range. She sounded just like a young man in his twenties, which was who she'd told them she was. Not a woman in her mid-thirties.

"Victor! Jesus, you scared me. Don't sneak up on me like that." His dark, beady eyes examined her for a moment. "Did you hear any of that?"

She shrugged. "Just sounded like someone at the other warehouse fucked up."

"You could say that." He pushed back his chair and walked to where she stood in the doorway. "We're about to get a very important shipment, and I need someone to help guard it. Are you interested in the extra hours?"

"Of course." Could this be her big break?

"Now, this is our most important line of business, so you won't be able to talk to anyone about it. It's top secret."

"Yes, sir." Thank God her voice didn't waver.

"Alright, I'll add you to the schedule. See you tomorrow."

"See you tomorrow, Norm." She locked her face into a calm determination as she strode away, but inside she was shaking with anticipation. "Victor" had finally earned his place and she would get to peek behind the curtain.

And then Violet was going to blow it wide open for all to see.

She slipped up the back staircase, going up all the way to the roof via the service entrance. Last time, she'd gotten a great view of the water from the roof. But today, the clouds had rolled in and lightning cracked across the black sky. Normally she had to be careful no one was up here for a smoke break, but she was the only one crazy enough to come up during a storm.

Probationary employees weren't allowed phones? With living on the premises, Violet wasn't sure about the legality of that. Thank God she'd ended up buying two burners and had an extra to hand over when Norm prompted her for it. But she still had the second. She just couldn't get caught breaking the rules or this whole operation would go sideways. She propped the door open with a rock someone had left and pulled her hood up over her head while making her way over to the giant air conditioning unit along the edge she always used to shield herself. Slipping her phone out of her pocket, she dialed Wanda's number and shivered while she waited for her to pick up the phone.

"Violet! How's it going?"

She practically had to yell to be heard over the wind. Good thing she was alone. "Hey, Wanda. Uh, I'm not sure how to say this, but I uncovered something today that makes me really nervous."

"What's wrong?"

She didn't have much time. Just a few seconds outside and she was already soaked to the bone. "It turns out that NT is part of a trafficking ring."

"Jesus Christ on a pogo stick! Violet, you gotta get out of there!"

Violet shook her head, not that Wanda could see her. She'd thought about her options on the walk up the stairs. "If I leave now, it'll look suspicious. Plus, I don't have any hard evidence to prove it, just a conversation I overheard. But I don't know what to do." She wiped the rain out of her eyes. "This is bigger than anything I've ever uncovered before."

"Are you sure you're safe? You could end up trafficked!"

"Trust me, Wanda, I'm safe." She hadn't told Wanda her fake identity, and now wasn't the time. She needed to get out of the storm.

"Remember, if you miss two check ins, I'm sending someone in for you. And if they find out who you are, you get the fuck out of Dodge, you understand me?"

"I understand." And she'd do whatever it took not to leave. This story had buried itself in her heart with a new urgency. She had to get eyes on the women and get them help.

"I'll talk to you Saturday night."

"You got it, Wanda." Just as she hung up the call, an emergency alert blasted her eardrum. She cried out in shock and her phone slipped from her hand.

Violet watched, frozen in horror as it bounced on the edge of the wall surrounding the flat warehouse roof. She reached for it, but she was too slow. The phone escaped her wet grasp and went up over the wall, disappearing into the watery void below.

Her heart pounded as she leaned over into the storm. The rain plastered her hair to her head, and the glue for the fake beard had started to let go. But Violet just stared into the darkness, where her lifeline to the world had disappeared.

Chapter 7

"Roll a D8 for damage, Josie."

As Finn's girl rolled her eight-sided die, Jon rolled his own dice behind the Dungeon Master's screen. Usually Roger ran their campaigns, but this time Jon had had an idea that wouldn't let go. It was fun, but sometimes he wished he could go back to playing around and seducing all the NPCs as a bard. This was a lot of work.

Oh, crap. Josie's spell had triggered his villain's trap, but also damaged the villain. He did some quick math in his head and realized after all the other damage the party had wrought that the witch was dead.

"Six."

"Okay, you take six hit points of damage, because there was a booby trap spell on the cottage. But your spell got through and the witch is dead."

Cheers went up around the table. Jon's little brother, Finn, leaned over to give Josie a kiss.

"Gross, Bro. Save it for later," he teased.

Finn just flipped him the bird with a smug grin.

"Okay, they said we have to bring them her head, so let's get to it. Chop chop." Jenna, Roger's bloodthirsty redhead, rubbed her hands together.

Roger just chuckled. "Alright little Amazon, I'm the barbarian, so I guess that's my job."

After the party had gone back to the town victorious, Jon brought out the snacks and beer. His first time hosting the game session had been a success, and he couldn't wait to continue the campaign.

"So, when are we doing this again?" He took a pull from his bottle.

"Hold that thought." Roger wandered away from the table as his phone lit up with a call. "Hunt Security, Roger speaking." He answered the call out in the hallway.

"Maybe when Josie and I get back from our trip?" Finn wrapped his right arm around Josie's shoulders, the light on his bionic prosthetic shining.

"Where are you going?" Jon raised an eyebrow.

"He's taking me on a road trip." Josie wrapped the arm closest to her man around his waist as Finn looked down.

"We're going to go see my unit."

Ahh. Finn had ended up the sole survivor of that roadside bomb and hadn't been able to travel for anyone's funeral because of his own injuries. Jon nodded in understanding.

"I've always wanted to see the country, so we'll take our time and see the sights."

Finn smiled. "Vasquez used to talk about the Grand Canyon, so we're definitely going there."

They gazed fondly at each other, and Jon rubbed at a spot on his chest that suddenly grew tight. He'd never begrudge his brothers their happiness, but damn, he wanted some of his own.

Roger came back into the dining room and hung up his call. "Hey guys, we need to get home and do a virtual consult with a potential client. She's got an urgent thing she needs help with. Jon, you in?"

"Sure." Why wouldn't he be in? This was why he'd joined Roger's team. Finally, some action!

"Great. We better get going. I told her I'd call her as soon as possible."

"Alright, I'll meet you there." Josie and Jenna helped him put away the food. Then everyone put their shoes on and trooped over to Roger's house, Jon following his older brother's Chevy in his own truck.

Sam and Frankie met them at the house, and Roger directed them into the living room where he'd set up his smart TV with the video camera. "She's in Virginia, but she's my old commanding officer's sister, so she contacted us. These two have got the network tied down tight, so I don't have to worry about hackers."

"Helps when you employ one." Jon chuckled. Frankie grinned and settled in next to Sam. Josie bid them good night and excused herself upstairs to study.

Roger brought up his video conferencing app and dialed. The screen opened up to an older woman, about fifty, with salt and pepper hair cut in a neat bob. She sat at a desk with framed magazine articles on the wall behind her. "Hello, Roger."

"Hi, Wanda. This is my team." He gave a quick round of introductions.

"Jay spoke highly of you and Sam. Nice to meet you all. I just wish this was under better circumstances." Wanda sighed.

Roger leaned forward and Jon could see how he'd blended his protective spirit with his business mindset. "What's going on, Wanda? How can we help?"

"I'm an editor at InVestigate Magazine. I run the business department, meaning my writers expose shady business practices. Some of them like to go undercover, and while it's not my favorite method, I can't really ignore the results."

"Sounds dangerous."

"It can be. And I'm worried that my best reporter bit off more than she can chew." The screen changed to show a photo of a woman with dark hair and fathomless deep brown eyes next to Wanda's face.

Jon's spine snapped straight. He'd recognize Ramona anywhere.

"This is Violet Giordano. She went undercover to investigate the shipping company Nautical Transit. Some concerned citizens of the town they operate in wrote us and indicated something shady was going on. I trust Violet. She's done this before. Maybe you saw her article on a drug ring running in Annapolis out of a bar? But the last I heard from her, she indicated this was much bigger than we were led to believe."

"Nautical Transit. Why do I know that name?" Frankie murmured.

"Because it's one of the syndicate's shell companies." Sam had his tablet out and was scrolling madly through it. He stopped and pointed at something on the screen. "There. It's in your notes from the shipping manifests."

"Shit." Frankie chewed at her nail.

"The syndicate? The same people who had…" Jon lifted his gaze to the ceiling, not wanting to say Josie's name. Sam and Frankie nodded. He stole a glance at Finn on Roger's other side, his fists clenched tight.

Roger tilted his head to the side. "Did she tell you what she thought they're up to?"

"She said they were trafficking women." Wanda swallowed and bit her lip. "I'm terrified, Roger. She's missed two check-ins and I fear the worst."

"How long has it been since you heard from her?"

"Ten days."

Connections were firing in Jon's head at a rapid rate. A drug ring running in a bar in Annapolis? That sounded like their old haunt. But he hadn't moved up in rank by assuming he was right.

"Wanda, did she get the Rusty Nail shut down?"

The older woman preened. "I suppose you could say she did. That was her best work. She even won an award for that piece."

Suddenly everything clicked into place. Ramona's desire for privacy, her disappearance… she'd been undercover. And now she was undercover again, but Ramona… no,

Violet... had uncovered sex traffickers. If they'd discovered she wasn't who she said she was, the syndicate wouldn't just kill her. No, they'd *sell* her. The vibrant woman he'd fallen for years ago would be a shell of her former self if she didn't get out of there, and fast.

He tamped down the anger that threatened to rise, leftover from his realization she'd disappeared without a word. It didn't matter if it had all been an act. If fucking him had been part of her cover, he'd still be going in there. She didn't deserve this fate when she was just trying to do her job. And she was damn good at it too, from what he remembered happening with The Rusty Nail Saloon.

"Take the job," Jon spoke low in Roger's ear. "I'm doing it."

Roger eyed him suspiciously, but he nodded. "Send me as much information as you have, Wanda. We'll work on a plan to extract her."

"Thank you, Roger. The email's on its way."

"We'll be in touch." They said their goodbyes and signed off. That's when Roger turned to Jon. "What's your plan?"

"I'll go undercover the same way Ramon — I mean, Violet — did."

"What did you call her?" Jenna asked, her face scrunched in confusion.

Jon sighed and hung his head. "Four years ago, I had a … thing with a woman who told me her name was Ramona. We met at the Rusty Nail. She disappeared on me without a word one day and I didn't see her again… until Wanda showed us that picture on the screen."

Roger leaned back against the couch. "Holy shit."

"Yeah. Holy shit is right." Jon ran a hand through his hair.

"Hang on, let me get this straight. You have history with her, so you want to play Captain Save-a-Ho?" Jenna asked.

"It's just Lieutenant Save-a-Ho, you couldn't pay me enough to be a Captain." Jon sniped back. "And she's not a hooker."

Jenna waved him off. "It's just an expression."

"He's the only one we can spare, Jenna." Roger looked at his girlfriend. "Think about it. The syndicate knows my face. I'm *not* sending you or Frankie in there. We need Sam for the cyber security clients. And Finn is already assigned to Josie's detail."

"Plus, you don't have enough bail money to send me in there." Finn squeezed his left fist with the hand of his bionic arm.

Sam chuckled. "Yeah, we can't afford to send anyone but Jon."

"I'm not criticizing!" Jenna raised her hands in defeat. "It was just a question."

"Maybe don't call her a ho when you're asking questions," Frankie spat, crossing her arms over her chest. "That sistah is in there trying to do in a matter of weeks what we haven't been able to do in months or even years. And she didn't have half the intel we got going in." She glared at her friend, and even Jon winced internally. "She's one of us and she don't even know it."

Roger clapped his hands. "Alright. We need an extraction plan."

"We don't know enough yet. Once I have an address, I can get the blueprints for the building." Sam pushed his glasses up his nose.

"And I'll hack the security cameras." Frankie grinned.

Roger stood from the couch. "I'll add the files to the shared drive. Every day counts with something like this."

Frankie tapped him on the shoulder. "Pick a new last name, hotshot. I'll work on your fake identification while I wait."

Jon gave her a cocky salute. "How about Stallone?"

"Too obvious." She shook her black curls. "Try something more common."

"John White."

"With the H?"

"Yeah, let's make it easy."

"You got it." She held out her sepia-toned hand. "Gimme your license so I can get the photo right."

He pulled out his wallet and slapped the plastic into her palm when Roger called out from the office.

"Sending the files now. Jon, you should come read this."

"Roger that!" Jon smirked, knowing his brother was rolling his eyes. Finn snickered and gave him a fist bump, while Frankie and Sam disappeared up the stairs.

"Haven't had a chance to use that lately, good one."

"Thanks." He slapped Finn on the shoulder. "If I don't get to see you off, have fun on the trip."

"We will." They went their separate ways, Finn up to see his girl, and Jon back to Roger's office.

His older brother sat with his elbows on the desk, his hands folded in front of his chin, glaring at the screen. "I don't like this."

"What is it?"

Roger waved him behind the desk to look at the monitor. "According to the notes Wanda sent over, the townspeople said they never saw anyone leave the building, and that prompted the investigation. From what Violet told her before her disappearance, they insist employees live in the dorms on the top two floors."

"That's weird as fuck." And shady, too, if they didn't trust their own people.

Roger shook his head. "You sure about this?"

Jon swallowed the lump in his throat as he recalled Violet's image on the screen. He remembered her sharp wit, their movie marathons, and the age-old argument about whether *Die Hard* was a Christmas movie. The name suited her far better than Ramona ever did. Switching it in his head felt natural. And thinking of her in danger brought his feelings for her roaring back to the surface. "I'm sure."

"Alright. Go upstairs and talk to Sam about how you're going to apply to this without giving them our IP address. Then you better run home and pack a bag."

"You got it."

"And Jon?"

Jon turned around in the doorway to face his brother. Roger had a serious look on his face that he hadn't seen since Finn got home from the Marines.

"We've been working with one of Sam's friends at the Bureau who's trying to bring these guys down. They're the scum of the Earth. If you get anything we can use, send it on."

Jon lifted his right arm in a salute. "Yes, sir."

FINALLY, VIOLET WAS OUT on the floor and away from the tight quarters of Norm's office. "Victor" was doing the work he'd been hired to do. Moving boxes. Unmarked boxes.

Her arms nearly shook with the exertion from her day. But the comments calling her "shrimp" and "kid" had only ensured she'd stuck it out. After all, she couldn't afford to blow her cover now that she knew what Nautical Transit really shipped.

"Did you see that guy back there?" Billy Bob's voice came from the other side of the aisle, talking to another guy whose name she hadn't retained. His conversation partner only grunted. "He's almost as pretty as a woman."

Her stomach dropped. Were they talking about her? Fuck, fuck, fuck.

"You gay, Billy Bob?" The other man sneered.

"Hell naw! I just meant if you put him in a dress, he could *almost* be a chick."

Violet breathed a silent sigh of relief, not stopping her movements. Fuck, why hadn't she made Victor a certified forklift driver?

But she'd miss conversations like these and she knew it.

Billy Bob's so-called friend continued to tease and call him gay slurs until Billy Bob had enough.

"I ain't no homo, Xan! You know it ain't up to us what clients want."

She stilled again, theatrically wiping sweat from her brow. They weren't talking about her.

Wait. The merchandise was more than just women?

"I still don't think we should be catering to *fags*." The other NT worker spat in disgust. Then he muttered something under his breath that she didn't catch, but he made a sound that sounded like a gun firing.

Her lunch threatened to come back up, but she stuffed it down. As the two men walked away, their footsteps echoing in the warehouse, a memory from childhood assaulted her.

"It's my turn to play the princess!" Callum said, his hands grabbing for her yellow Belle gown.

"But I'm not done yet!" Violet pouted, her arms wrapping around her favorite piece of her dress-up collection. She pulled Aurora's dress from her chest, knowing it was Cal's favorite. "Why don't we both be princesses?"

"Okay," he acquiesced quickly. He pulled the plastic armor off, tossing it everywhere, then pulled the dress over his head. They did each other's make up with her Cinderella

palette, then had themselves a little tea party. When Mama came to get them for dinner, she slapped her hand over her forehead.

"Children, your father will be home soon. It's time to clean up."

"But Mom, I want to be a princess some more!" Cal whined.

"Callum, you cannot let your father see you like this," she said as she pulled him to his feet and started pulling the pink polyester from over his head. "Now come into the bathroom and wash your face."

They'd never discussed it out loud, but based on her mother's reaction to Callum's feminine side, Violet suspected her father of being a homophobe. Wasn't it lucky then, that Callum hadn't hit puberty yet when Dad died? How different would their lives have been if their dad had lived through that work accident?

Then the penny dropped. She was no safer here as Victor than Callum had been playing dress-up with her as a child. Her skin grew clammy despite her sweatshirt. But it was too late to back out now. She'd known that when she overheard Norm talking about the merchandise. If she left now, they'd hunt her down for what she knew. He'd made it very clear that whatever happened at Nautical Transit stayed there.

THREE WEEKS OF WAITING and wondering if Ramona — no, *Violet* — was okay. Three weeks of searching for her work online and reading all the articles she'd ever written. Jon had learned so much about her from her writing. And he'd needed that connection to her. He hadn't known Ramona, not really. But he felt as though he'd caught a glimpse into the woman behind her. And he was even more drawn to her than he was four years ago.

He tamped down the nervous energy that asked if she was okay. Whatever had happened, he'd be there to help her deal with it, if she wanted him to be.

Finn pulled up to the warehouse, his hat pulled low over his brow. "Be safe, brother."

"You know it." They'd opted for Finn to drive Jon down because they couldn't afford for anyone to run the plate on his truck if he left it in the parking lot. Since the syndicate didn't know Finn's face, he was deemed the best choice. "Don't worry. I'll get her out, and we'll fry these fuckers."

"Word." They bumped their fists together and Jon jumped out of Finn's F-150 with his duffel bag slung over his shoulder.

They'd used Frankie's connection to the syndicate servers to get his interview. Honestly, Norm had no idea where he'd come from but he apparently had issues with his warehouse staff and he needed the help. Hopefully he didn't dig too deep at the fake references, since they wouldn't know his alter ego, John White, from Adam.

He yanked on the industrial door and greeted the security guard inside.

"Welcome aboard. Norm's expectin' ya." The tall, beefy guard was more for show than anything. Jon doubted he was trained in anything but lifting weights. Jon slipped through the second door into the warehouse proper.

The two-story room was a yellow cinderblock echo chamber, with what amounted to an observation deck around the upper floor. Two guys stood next to each other, drinking a beer and shooting the shit. Everyone in the vicinity stopped and stared at him, and at Norm striding across the ancient tile floor.

"John! Great to have you aboard!" The older man shook his hand. Several of the guys gathered around to nod at the new guy. "Everyone, this is John White. He's our new recruit."

"Nice to meet you." He'd sized Norm up at their interview. Typical graying middle-aged manager type, with the large gut from sitting at a desk and giving orders. If

Jon hadn't known better from the get go, he'd never have thought there was anything shady going on.

Although the lack of women would have thrown him off. Even the most macho organizations had finally had to bow down to include women in the workforce at some point in the last ten years, even if they didn't make it easy on them.

"Yo, Vic!" Norm called up to the guys standing at the railing. "Meet me in my office." The shorter, younger-looking dude with black hair and a goatee raised his bottle in acknowledgment. He looked like he should be stepping onto a stage with an all-male pop group with that hair, not wearing baggy hoodies and working at a warehouse.

He disappeared from the railing and Jon followed Norm back through the hallway to his office.

"Have a seat, John." Jon settled his bag at his feet as he sat down in the uncomfortable plastic chair.

"Now, since you're already familiar with the organization, coming from one of our sister companies, we've decided not to put you on probation."

Jon wasn't sure what he meant by probation, but he nodded anyway. Apparently, it didn't apply to him.

"I've got your paperwork all here, just sign..." Footsteps down the hall interrupted their conversation. He wrote his fake signature just as the young guy from the second floor appeared at the door.

"Vic! Come in and meet your new roommate. John, this is Victor. You two are going to room together." Norm waved between them. "You're no longer the new kid on the block, Vic."

Jon gave Victor a nod. He didn't look happy at the intrusion. Who would be? Jon hadn't had to share a room since the Academy, not that anyone here would know that.

"Nice to meet you." He stood and extended his hand. Victor looked at his offered hand for a second too long, then begrudgingly shook it.

A jolt of lightning took him by surprise. Those hands were small, and too soft to have been working in a warehouse for long. "You, too." He withdrew before Jon was ready. Was he ... was he suddenly attracted to men? Shit, this was the worst timing.

Victor waved him forward. "Come on, I'll show you around."

Chapter 8

VIOLET HAD WANTED TO be wrong. She'd thought maybe she'd seen someone else from her second-floor perch. Misheard his voice. But, no. The tall new guy with chestnut hair and a muscular frame was Jonathon Hunt. *Her* Jon. After seeing him face to face, she had no doubts. Her knees almost buckled beneath her as she shook his hand.

"I want both of you down here when the new shipment gets in tomorrow. It's initiation time," Norm added.

"Initiation?" She couldn't help the confused look on her face. The "merchandise" as Norm called them, had been moved out under cover of night after a few days in the warehouse before a new set was brought in. She was getting a much clearer picture of how the operation worked.

Boats came in at night only, and NT's victims didn't stay long. While she wasn't able to give them any comfort, she tried not to scare them too much. Just enough to convince her coworkers that she was on their side.

"Yep. You'll see." He gave her a smarmy grin then waved them on. "Get out of here for now."

"Sure, boss."

As they walked through the maze of hallways, Violet pointed out things like the entrance to the dock and the cafeteria, making their way up the building to her, now their, room on the fourth floor. She introduced Jameson as she passed him, the other man giving them both a nod as they continued on their way.

Did Jon know what this company was doing? She'd been held at arm's length because she came in here thinking they were a legitimate shipping business. Apparently if you knew about the trafficking coming in you were treated better.

If she'd known about the fucking trafficking, she wouldn't be here at all.

"Group bathrooms? Damn, it's like college all over again."

In her position, it sucked. She walked a delicate tightrope. Her water-resistant wig glue held up fine as long as her shower wasn't too hot. She did her best to use the communal bathroom at odd times, so no one would discover she never used the urinal. The tiny shower stalls were straight out of a gym, but at least they offered her privacy. Most of the guys weren't shy and changed in front of each other though, so she still had to be careful. More than one person had given her funny looks when she changed clothes inside the shower. So far, they'd shrugged it off.

"Yeah, it ain't too bad." She'd made sure Victor's speech pattern differed from her own. Then she pointed at a door. She'd spent most of the tour with her back to Jon, but now she had to face him. All. The. Time. "This is us." Stepping back, she gestured at the lock. "Let's check that your key works."

"Good idea." He slipped the key into the knob and turned. It opened. And just like that, Violet's safe space in this hell was gone.

She sat on the bed while Jon set up his half of the nondescript room, surreptitiously trying to ensure none of her stuff was sitting out that would give her away. Her dresser was a mess, but she snatched the bottle of wig glue up and slipped it into a drawer while he emptied his bag into his own set of drawers. She blew out a relieved breath. That was close.

Jon tried to make conversation. "Where are you from?"

"New York," was her curt reply.

She still couldn't wrap her head around him being here at all. The longer she stayed in his presence, the angrier she got. He figured out "Victor" wasn't in a talking mood pretty quickly and continued to unpack in silence, which meant she stewed with her thoughts. Then Jon pulled out a towel and a plastic basket of toiletries.

"I'm gonna grab a shower."

"See you." She opened the science fiction book she'd brought with her. It wasn't her usual genre, but she knew better than to bring a romance book when she was supposed to be masquerading as a dude.

At least it had a romantic subplot between the space pirate and the kidnapped queen. She loved the enemies-to-lovers trope, and this one had it in spades between the political maneuvers and space battles.

She'd gotten maybe ten pages further when Jon strode back into the room, totally naked except for the towel. Fuck, her memories of his body must have faded in four years, because she didn't remember how cut he was. A few drops of water cling to his abs and she fought the urge to lick her lips. He ignored her, standing in front of his dresser.

"What do y'all do for fun around here?"

Shit, she was ogling her roommate. And he was about to whip that towel off. There was no way she'd be able to keep up this act if she saw that tight, firm ass in person again.

Violet buried her face in her book with a finger holding her spot. She prayed her voice didn't shake. "Not much. I'm on probation so I can't use my phone."

"Shit, that sucks." Fabric rustled as he changed for bed. "I wondered what Norm was talking about when he said I didn't need to be on probation. Usually, it's just where they can fire you for any reason, right?"

"This ain't most places."

An idea occurred to her. While Jon was new, as roommates they were going to be spending a lot more time together than she spent with the other guys. She had a chance to get to know him well enough for him to think they'd be friends. "You don't s'pose I could borrow yours? My sister's gonna be pissed I haven't called. It's been weeks."

For the first time, Jon hesitated. "Sorry, I get horrible reception out here. Gotta update my plan once I get paid, so I can get a better network."

She nodded at his excuse, but she knew the truth. His reception was probably fine. He just didn't want to share with a stranger. Because it was obvious from his reactions that he thought she was an actual man.

He yawned and made his way into his bed in nothing but his boxer briefs. Dear God, have mercy. She was going to be affected. There was no way around it.

"You know the shipments don't come in until later in the day, right?" Her sleep schedule had gone to hell in a hand basket over the course of this assignment.

"I've been traveling all day and I'm beat. I can probably sleep with the light on."

Even she wouldn't be that cruel. "Nah, man. I'll go read elsewhere." At least that would give her space.

"Night."

"Good night." She flipped the light switch as she strode out their door.

The chairs in the kitchen weren't super comfortable, but she put two together so she could put her feet up like a recliner, and it would do. She checked her watch, grateful for the hundredth time that she'd thought to bring it. It was part of her costume, a twenty-dollar sport watch with an alarm that saved her bacon when her phone flew out of her hand. Without it, she'd have had to beg Norm for time off to go buy an alarm clock. She should have done it anyway, but she'd been in a dangerous position where he'd only just started to trust her. If he thought she'd be on her way to the authorities, she didn't want to think about what he'd do. And this initiation tomorrow indicated she was right to wait. They still hadn't trusted her, not fully.

She settled into her chair and opened her book, finding the scene where she'd left off. It was a good one, too, the space pirate finally realizing he was attracted to the queen from the other planet. But as she read, the images in her head of the characters warped. The pirate suddenly looked a lot like Jon, his muscles gleaming under the harsh light of their dorm room. And the queen no longer had purple hair, her own dark tresses taking their place.

He drew his fingers through her silken hair. "Atas'ha, you're…"

She huffed. "Arrogant? Controlling? Come now, Captain, you've never failed to tell me exactly what you think of me before." Her lower lip trembled as she stared into his eyes.

But in Violet's mind, those eyes were moss green, not blue like the hero's. And when the captain cupped her face and kissed her, she could feel Jon's mouth on hers.

She slapped the receipt she'd been using as a bookmark into the book and slammed it on the table. God damn it, she couldn't escape him even in fiction!

This was insane. She wouldn't let a guy get between her and her career. Not after watching her mother die without fulfilling her dreams. Like the old song, no one was going to drag her up to get into the life she deserved. Plus, she couldn't accept a man that would work with this company knowingly. The mere fact he'd already admitted he wasn't on probation meant he knew more than she had coming in. Violet rubbed her hand over her eyes and debated getting a cold shower. That would solve part of her problem. The part where she was horny and couldn't do anything about it. It wouldn't change the fact she was unbearably attracted to her roommate, and that she couldn't ever be with him. It wouldn't solve the problem that Wanda was probably going out of her mind and she didn't dare ask to borrow a phone from basically anyone else in this building.

Getting a hold of Jon's phone was her only hope to call out. But Jon didn't trust her. As well he shouldn't. Because this time when her story hit, he would go down in flames.

THE NEXT MORNING, JON woke up well before Victor. In deference to his roommate, he quietly slipped on clothes in the dark and made his way to the bathroom to brush his teeth and shave.

He didn't understand why Victor was so cold to him. Everyone else had seemed friendly when he showed up first for his interview and then when Norm hired him.

And suspiciously, his phone hadn't been where he left it when he went to bed last night. He didn't want to hide it under his pillow and potentially set his bed on fire, but after Vic had asked to use it and he blamed a bad network, he didn't think the guy would try to steal it in his sleep. Maybe he was too naïve, officer housing having made him soft. But it was clear he couldn't trust Victor.

The more he talked to Norm yesterday, the more he worried about Violet. He'd wondered out loud about the lack of diversity in the organization, but Norm had just chuckled. "Women don't fit into the operation at the same level you and I do," he'd said. Jon had laughed it off, playing his role, but he also knew the truth about these assholes.

He went downstairs for breakfast and listened to the other guys hanging out around the table. While he acted like their locker room talk didn't bother him, in reality the way they were talking about their 'merchandise' made his blood boil.

"That blonde sucked better than a Hoover."

"Did you see those tits on the redhead?"

Did none of these men have sisters? Mothers? Aunts? How would they feel if that was their daughter someone was talking about? But over eggs and bacon that tasted like ash in his mouth, he realized these men didn't see their victims as people. He also overheard them talking about male victims, how some of the customers wanted young, virile men to sate their desires. So no, it wasn't only girls that were being trafficked, but boys, too.

Sam had told him as much when they talked over beers one night. He admitted when he'd staked out the house where they rescued Josie, he'd seen someone take a young man out of the house with his hands bound and drive away. He'd admitted all the addresses were written in code, a code they had yet to break. Sam hoped they could get the young man and all the other victims back once they had that figured out.

His brother's friend had worked for the FBI, so he had connections that could make everything legal, but Jon didn't have time for the red tape that would involve. Frankly, none of the victims had time for it, but at least once he found Violet, he could get her out and send in the cavalry.

That was the plan, at least. Jon just had to find the stomach to handle what he needed to do.

Fuck.

With hours to go until the shipment came in and he and Victor had to report, he was bored out of his mind. Games on his phone were the only option, but he had to talk to someone. He just couldn't do it where he'd be overheard.

Stepping outside wasn't forbidden, but most of them avoided it. Six of the guys sat around playing cards, but he didn't feel like talking to these assholes any longer than necessary. His feet wandered until he came to the stairwell. That's when he had the idea of heading up to the roof. Would anyone notice?

He passed a couple of guys coming down the stairs, nodding as they passed each other. Jon *should* be learning their names, so he could turn them in when it came time to talk to the authorities. But his mind wasn't on the yahoos working for the syndicate. It was on Violet.

Four years since he'd last tasted those firm, mouth-sized tits. Four years since he'd run his hands through her black silken hair. Four years since he'd whisked her onto what passed for a dance floor at the Rusty Nail, her laughter as he entertained her with his boy band dance moves.

"Are you sure you're straight?"

"Hey, I was the most popular guy in middle school once the girls saw this routine. I was drowning in phone numbers."

The way her eyes turned to liquid chocolate when he drew her in for a slow song. The way his heart fluttered in his chest when he kissed her for the first time outside the diner, soft and slow.

Before he realized it, Jon found himself at the top of the stairwell, looking at a door marked "Roof Access". It definitely locked from the outside, but the rock on the floor next to it told him other people used this door. He'd have to be careful while he talked to his brother.

He propped the door open and slipped outside, taking in the view for the first time. They were on the shore, the red brick building hanging out over the water so the boats could come and go unseen. The flat roof was littered with cigarette butts, with a giant air conditioning unit on the far-right corner. From this vantage point, Jon could see almost the entire small town. Off in the distance stood the town square, with its shops and town hall. The funny thing he'd always heard about small towns was that everyone knew everyone else's business, so the fact that the syndicate would try to use it for their nefarious purposes confused him. Either someone wasn't playing with a full deck, or thought these people were dumb hicks.

It was a good thing they weren't. But then, if they had been, Violet wouldn't be in danger right now.

You idiot. She'd just find another story.

He'd pulled up the Rusty Nail article again while he waited to get hired at Nautical Transit, reading it with a new perspective. Violet's bravery and her integrity stood out in her writing. No wonder she'd won an award for it. Then he'd looked up what happened to their old haunt, reading over the news stories from when the DEA raided and shut it down. She'd done that. She'd taken hundreds of pounds of drugs off the street and made that tiny corner of Annapolis safer.

We need more people like her.

He rubbed at his chest as he thought about her. Was she holed up in some awful house, forced into sex slavery? Or had she gotten away and just not been able to contact Wanda? How the hell had she gotten in here as a woman, anyway?

So many questions and no answers.

His first step would be to talk to the women these assholes were selling. If they'd talk to him. Talk about needing a charisma bonus. He'd have to figure out how to gain their trust without setting off the suspicions of the syndicate goons. Which was why he could *not* let Victor get a hold of his phone.

He had messages from Roger on that burner, and Sam had installed a tracking chip just in case. If either of those were discovered, he was dead. Jenna and Frankie had explained that only through a lot of planning, and Frankie tampering with records, were they able to get away. Neither of them had even known of the syndicate's human trafficking ring until they'd left the organization. The girls had warned him if they caught him, he wouldn't be so lucky.

Finn and Josie were already on their road trip, so he dialed Finn's phone. "Hey, you. How's it going?"

"It's going fine so far. Just wanted to talk to you, that's all."

"We just stopped to stretch our legs. Josie's in the ladies' room."

"Where are you guys?"

"Stopped at a rest stop outside Pittsburgh." Finn paused. "You okay?"

Jon released a sigh. "I don't know." He scrubbed a hand over his face. "I just keep thinking, wondering what's happened to her."

"Don't let it get to you. You guys put a plan together. You just have to execute it."

He groaned. "There are a lot of unknowns, still. Like, there are no women in this building. None. I don't understand how she got in here."

"You'll have to ask when you find her."

"I know, it's just... what if I can't?" He squeezed his eyes shut, hating that he was so anxious about this. As an ex-Special Forces soldier, Roger would have been a better fit, but as he'd explained, the syndicate already knew his face and wouldn't be fooled. Jon had never been on this type of operation in the Navy, so while he was definitely thankful for the action, he also felt a bit out of his depth. And Violet's life was at stake!

"None of that. You will. The longer you're there, the deeper you'll be allowed to go. It's going to take time."

"She might not have time."

"Josie lasted six months. And Violet at least had some warning, enough to get a message to Wanda. You might have more time than you think."

"God, I hope so."

Finn said something Jon couldn't quite hear, then he came back to the phone. "Hey, Josie's back. She wants to talk to you."

"Did you tell her what's going on?"

"Of course. We have no secrets." His brother muffled the microphone with his hand and murmured something in the background. "Here she is."

Josie's sweet voice was the next one to come over the phone. "Hey, stranger."

"Hey. How's your cross-country road trip?"

"It's fantastic. Listen, Finn said you're worried about Violet, but she's older, right?"

"Her file said she's thirty-five." Come to think of it, they'd never discussed ages when they first met. He'd been surprised; he'd thought she was much younger than him.

"It probably won't be as bad as you think. This type of ordeal's harder on the younger ones. I was able to compartmentalize the experience, according to my therapist. And I'm twenty-five. I hope that helps."

"A little. Thanks." He almost said Josie's name, then thought better of it. Just in case someone came up the stairs.

"I'll pass you back to Finn."

"Hey, Brother. What are you thinking?"

Jon let out a breath, eyeing the staircase over his shoulder. "I'm thinking get her out, but don't rush it. If I rush it, I might get sloppy, and that will put the operation in danger."

"Sounds solid. Hang in there, okay? Do what you have to."

"You got it, jarhead. Take care of that girl, okay? You lucky bastard."

He could hear Finn's grin through the phone. "Always. Love you, squid."

"Love you, too." He hung up the phone and enjoyed the peaceful sunshine for a while longer before the cold February air drove him back into the warm building.

Checking the time, he realized there were hours to go before he and Victor were due to report for their initiation. If this place ran on night owl hours, he'd need a nap to help reset his internal clock. He headed back down the stairs after securing the door and the rock. The door to his room opened, and he watched Victor walking down the hall. Victor didn't see him. Jon was tempted to call out, to make friends with the guy, since they were going to be living together. And the more friends he made here, the more trustworthy he'd look. But something about this guy just rubbed him the wrong way, and he didn't want something to happen to his phone during his nap.

Victor would be the one most likely to catch him if he slipped up.

So, Jon waited until Victor disappeared down the other stairwell, the one without roof access. And then he slipped into their room.

He stripped down to his boxers and set an alarm on his phone. Then he turned the light out and slid under the covers. He'd almost gotten to sleep when the click of the door jolted him wide awake. But he kept his eyes closed. He wanted to see what Victor would do if he thought he was asleep.

The door clicked shut almost silently. He had to give Victor credit. Jon couldn't hear his feet across the tile floor, so he must have slipped his shoes off. But enough light came through the cracks in the blinds to cast a shadow when Victor stood next to his bed. Jon kept his breathing deep and even, feigning sleep. He lifted the corner of his lashes just enough to see as Victor reached for his phone on the nightstand. Then he struck.

His hand shot out from beneath the duvet and grabbed Victor's wrist, who jumped a mile. "Holy fuck!" His voice jumped high, like he'd hit puberty all over again.

"Don't touch my shit, asshole," Jon growled. Victor's wrist was tiny. He could probably snap it if he squeezed hard enough. But that would get him in trouble, and probably thrown out before he had a chance to find Violet. He couldn't risk it.

"Dude! I'm sorry."

"My phone is off-limits. I already told you last night you couldn't borrow it."

Victor cradled his wrist to his chest. "Jesus. You about gave me a heart attack."

"And you were going to use something of mine without permission!"

"I said I'm sorry." His face was flushed, and he raised his hands in the air.

Jon had enough. "Don't do it again. I won't be so nice next time." He put his arm back under the blanket and got comfortable again. "I'm trying to reset my sleep schedule since y'all are night owls here. I'll see you at initiation. And my phone better not get moved again."

"See you later." Victor stomped out of the room, grabbing his shoes and a book as he hightailed it out of their room with a sigh.

Jon rolled over and fell asleep for real, figuring that was the last he'd have to deal with *that* for a while.

Chapter 9

THE NEW SHIPMENT CAME in after dinner. Violet and Jon ate with the others, but no one else seemed to notice the tension between the two roommates. He really had scared the shit out of her, grabbing her wrist while he pretended to sleep. She hadn't remembered him being quite so harsh before. But it had been four years. And people changed, not always for the better.

Could her disappearance have caused him to hate women so much he joined a trafficking ring? Almost as soon as the thought formed, Violet dismissed it. She couldn't think like that. It wasn't her fault. She had to focus on her story, on her quest to expose Nautical Transit for their crimes.

She led Jon down to Norm's office, silence stretching between them. Jon was clearly pissed off, and he had every right to be, but she was getting desperate. Wanda had to be losing her mind.

Violet knocked on the doorjamb since Norm's door was open. "Ah, Victor, John. Right on time. Follow me."

She kept her expression blank, but inside she felt like she was being led to the gallows. Norm took them down the back hallway where Violet hadn't been allowed yet. These were rooms they sometimes put the victims in between trips. She hadn't known why, but she was about to find out.

"Your induction is simple. You get to sample the merchandise." His sleazy smile made Violet's stomach churn, and his words made her pulse pound. She could barely hear his next words over the whooshing sound in her ears. He pointed at two doors. "There you are, gentlemen. One for each of you."

As horrified as Violet was, this made sense. If they weren't willing to go through with it, NT would know they weren't really on their side. She'd be exposed as a traitor for sure. But she didn't have the equipment they were looking for! Norm slapped them both on the back at the same time and sent them forward. In a daze, she opened the door on the left and walked into the room.

It was bare bones, hardly a bedroom. A dirty mattress on a frame stood against the far wall, a skinny blonde girl in a threadbare sundress handcuffed to a ring in the wall. The poor thing looked to be about seventeen, malnourished, and she desperately needed a shower. She looked at Violet with wide blue eyes, and her lip began to quiver.

"Hey, hey, it's okay." Violet whispered and rushed to calm her. "I won't hurt you." The trembling subsided, but Violet knew she couldn't give the girl too much hope. "Look, I'm not... I can't let them find out I'm not actually into girls." She bit her lip. "If they find out, they'll kill me. Can you help me make this look good? Please?"

This could be her chance to show the victims they could trust her, so that they'd follow her. If she ever got a chance to get them out.

The young woman swallowed, reluctantly offering more information. "There's a guy back with the others..."

Violet shook her head. She wasn't here to abuse anyone. "I can't. The guys here are all homophobes and we live together." She bit her lip. They couldn't find out she wasn't a guy. "Please?"

The girl thought for the longest moment in Violet's life. Then she nodded. "Okay."

"What's your name?"

She rolled her eyes. "They don't ask that. Just yell at me to take it and shut up. And bang the bed against the wall." Then she took a deep breath and screamed. "No! No, stop!"

God, the strength of this girl. Violet slid down to the floor and shoved the bed repeatedly into the wall like she'd been told to. "Shut up and take it!" She grunted like a dude as the poor girl on the bed cried. Next door she could hear a similar banging sound and her heart broke. Because Jon was just like the rest of the guys here.

She fucking hated him.

But she channeled him when she pretended to come, as she heard him coming through the thin as fuck walls. Her theater arts teacher from high school would be proud of this performance. She gently touched the girl's foot, making the poor thing jolt. "Thank you," she said sincerely.

She just shrugged. "There'll be others." Then she looked Violet up and down. "Mess up your clothes, you look too neat."

Violet couldn't say anything without giving herself away, so she nodded and rumpled herself, running her hands over her hoodie and unbuttoning her jeans. She opened the door and sauntered out into the hall, doing up the button like she had just pulled her pants up.

Jon exited the same time, a satisfied grin on his face. Norm eyed them both. "Welcome to the syndicate."

Violet tilted her head. "Syndicate?"

Norm gave her that sleazy grin. "Nautical Transit's parent company, if you will. We are the shipping arm of the organization."

Holy shit. This sounded way bigger than she'd thought it would be. Had Violet finally bitten off more than she could chew?

Jon crossed his arms. "Didn't know you liked to listen in, Norm."

Norm shrugged. "Part of my duties. Now, you both get some rest. I have an assignment for you that means you have to leave early in the morning."

Of course. She'd become a night owl to deal with this job and now she'd have to get up early for it. Go figure.

"Sure thing, boss. What's the assignment?" Jon asked.

"I need you to go pick up a boat and bring it back here. Pack a bag, you'll have to sail through the night."

"Yes, sir." And it was Jon that led the way back to their dorm room, Violet seething all the way.

It occurred to her while they were heading up the stairs that Jon's girl hadn't cried out like hers had. Obviously, the poor things were used to getting assaulted regularly. Either Jon's had been around longer and given up hope, or ... he'd actually made it good for her. God, she hoped so. She'd been on the receiving end of his prowess in bed before, and he knew his way around a woman's body.

The cold silence descended once more as they moved through the warehouse. This was the craziest assignment she'd ever ended up on.

What have you gotten yourself into, Violet Marie? she thought to herself.

Violet felt grimy, like she wanted to crawl out of her skin thinking about that poor girl downstairs. Secrets be damned, she had to shower. Even if Jon was in the bathroom at the same time. She'd just change in the shower stall like she always did.

He didn't even pay attention when she followed him into the communal bathroom, though she did take the shower cubicle two down from him, to give herself some space. After scrubbing her skin raw, she dried off and got dressed in her pajamas before drawing the curtain back. Back in their room, she set the alarm on her watch and slid under her covers. Jon was already in bed, his back turned to her, facing his phone. She turned away from him as well, pissed as hell that he was here to begin with.

Her mind was wide awake, unable to relax with the thoughts of their upcoming road trip. Could she convince him to let her stop somewhere for a phone? She wasn't sure how strict Norm would be on their timeline.

Damn it, she was screwed.

Violet squeezed her eyes shut and tried to think of something else. Her thoughts went back to the teenager in that dirty bed. Brain bleach. That's what she'd need after this story was done. She was going to drink an entire bottle of whiskey once her article was finished. And then she'd buy one for Wanda since she'd be the one editing it.

And who was this syndicate anyway? Violet had more questions than answers now, thanks to Norm.

She buried her head under the blanket and prayed for sleep to come.

Jon lay awake, staring at his phone and waiting for Victor to fall asleep first. He didn't trust the guy not to try to steal it again.

While he waited, his mind drifted to the poor woman held against her will downstairs. She'd been confused when he entered the room and didn't take off his pants.

"Ugh, another one."

"Honey, I'm not going to fuck you," he'd whispered. "I have to make it sound good, so the boss thinks I am, but I won't touch you."

She'd furrowed her brow. "Why?"

"I'm not one of them. I'm just pretending." He hoped she understood how sincere he was. "I'm looking for someone. Someone they might have sold. Do you know a Violet?"

A slow shake of the head flipped her red curls around the mattress. "No, but they move us a lot."

"Thanks. Okay, let me make some noise and then I'll be out of your hair."

He'd overheard the exchange between Victor and his "sample", and he didn't know how he could ever look the man in the eye again. Unfortunate, since they were being forced into a road trip tomorrow. What kind of asshole actually said that shit to a woman? Jon's stomach churned, threatening to bring up dinner.

Once he'd been brought onto the team, Jenna had pulled him aside and explained how they discovered the syndicate's trafficking ring. She'd told him what terrible shape Josie had been in when they rescued her. She'd wanted to give him an idea of what to expect, so he didn't give himself away the minute he saw the victims.

Since he was awake anyway, Jon pulled his phone off the nightstand and send a message to Roger.

> **Jon: Getting a new boat tomorrow.**

> **Roger: Send more info when you have it.**

> **Jon: My roommate keeps trying to take my phone. Might have to go silent. He's coming with.**

> **Roger: Be careful.**

> **Jon: Night.**

Jon deleted the messages after confirming the last one went through. Some careful listening to Victor's breathing told him his roommate was asleep. Then he hid the phone in a drawer and silently pushed it shut.

Now it was time to try and sleep. Normally when he was this keyed up, he'd jack off, but his dick was the opposite of interested. He blamed that "initiation" but he'd done what he needed to do to keep up the ruse. It had worked, too. He was that much closer to finding Violet. And then he wanted answers to why she didn't trust him with the truth.

Hang on, Violet. I'm coming for you, sweetheart.

Chapter 10

MORNING CAME TOO EARLY. Violet stumbled through her morning routine, dabbing more wig glue under her beard. She'd need to take it off and reapply completely tonight. Hopefully Jon would be too distracted driving the boat, and she'd get some time to herself. It would hold for now.

Jon didn't speak a word as they grabbed breakfast and coffee. She was used to speaking in grunts with the guys, but Jon was wide awake and seemed lucid enough for conversation. Which meant he was ignoring her.

Good.

At least she could pretend she didn't hate him and blame the lack of caffeine on her surliness this morning. But that would have to go away once they got on the road. She'd have to attempt to be civil. It made her want to barf.

Jon's arrival had really thrown her. Violet had never had to fight herself so hard to keep her cover story than when it came to Jon. She'd nearly come clean four years ago, when they had initially met. But her professional integrity wouldn't let her. Her mother had given up her dreams, and Violet had sworn she never would make the same mistake. Now it was even more important to remind herself to maintain her cover. She was truly in the lion's den, and she didn't dare let them know she wasn't one of them. When she'd brainstormed what could be going on at Nautical Transit, organized crime hadn't actually hit her radar Neither had human trafficking. As pissed as she was that Jon had joined them, she couldn't scream and yell like she wanted to. She was Victor. Not Violet. Not here.

Norm found them in the cafeteria, staring into their cereal.

"You boys ready?"

"Sure, Norm."

"Who wants to drive the van?"

"We can take turns," Jon answered.

Violet agreed with a nod. "You can go first. You're more awake."

"Excellent. Here's the address. I'll leave you to it."

"And you want us to just leave the van?"

"Yep. One of the other businesses needs it, so they'll pick it up in Charleston."

"Gotcha." Jon finished his cereal off, pouring the bowl into his mouth. Violet looked away when she realized she was watching his Adam's apple bob as he swallowed.

It wasn't her fault he was still so attractive. How was she going to survive an entire day cooped up with him?

"Oh, Vic, I got your phone." Norm handed over a phone Violet didn't recognize.

She looked it over. "This isn't my phone." It wasn't the same burner she'd turned in, at least.

"It is for now. It's just for communicating with the team." Violet didn't dare argue as she pocketed the phone. But calling Wanda on a phone from the syndicate was out of the question. Who knew what kind of tracking they'd installed on this thing?

Norm nodded as if everything was settled. "Alright, I'll see you both tomorrow." With that, he walked away.

"You all set?" Jon asked her.

Violet gestured to the bag at her feet. "Ready when you are."

"Let's get this show on the road."

She dumped her dishes in the dishwasher because she wasn't a heathen, and he did the same. Then they each shouldered their duffel bags and headed down to the garage where NT stored their vans.

Jon clicked the button on the key fob and the lights for a nondescript white van flickered. Violet swallowed the comment that came to mind about it being a kidnapper van. That was way too close to the truth for this place.

"You don't suppose this thing has satellite radio, do you?" Jon spoke to her for the first time that morning.

Violet scoffed. "Doubt they'd spring for it."

"Good point." Jon unlocked the van, and they threw their bags into the back seat. Violet hurried into the passenger seat up front, not wanting to think about how many victims this van had transported behind her. He seemed completely unbothered, so she tried to feign nonchalance as well.

Jon programmed the address Norm had given them into the GPS mounted in the car. Then they were on their way.

"So, tell me about your sister."

Violet reacted before she could stop herself. "Sister?"

"Yeah, you said your sister would be pissed you hadn't called her since you lost your phone. Are you close?"

Violet didn't have a sister. Damn it! She'd been thinking of Wanda when she'd said that, but didn't dare give away why she was really here. "Uh, she's a … a performer." She should have come up with a cover story before this. Norm hadn't asked questions, and frankly she hadn't thought she'd still be here this long. But she could pretend her brother was her sister. She'd make this work.

"Really? What's her name?"

"Anita." Okay, Anita was Cal's drag name, but Jon wouldn't know that.

"She live around here?"

"Nah, she's still in New York. I don't get to see her much." That much was true.

"I gotcha."

"You got any brothers or sisters?" She remembered Jon talking at length about his siblings four years before. But she couldn't let on that she recalled his baby sister being in college or his brothers also being in the military.

"There's four of us. Three boys, and then one girl."

Violet chuckled. "Poor thing."

"Yeah, we didn't make life easy on her once she got old enough to date." He grinned. "But then she had us wrapped around her little finger basically from the day she was born, so I figure we're even."

They fell into a comfortable silence, an uneasy truce in Violet's mind. It didn't make sense how fondly Jon spoke of his sister when he was in the syndicate, knowingly transporting women against their will. But she couldn't afford to think about that, now. Three hours into the trip, though, her legs were stiff and her throat was dry as hell.

"Let's stop at the next rest stop. I need a drink."

"Sounds good. I need to take a piss." He steered the van to the right as the little blue sign popped up. After a winding driveway, a squat cement building came into view. The sun shone brightly, but she wasn't going to be deceived. It was still February and cold, no matter what the weather would have her believe.

Opening the van door, she jumped down, eager to walk around. Jon grunted as he hit the pavement. "Let's see what's on offer in the vending machines, too."

"Sounds good." She had thankfully brought some cash with her. It was getting low, since she didn't have access to her usual accounts, but it was enough for food for the road.

She pulled her coat around her tightly as they marched along the sidewalk to the public rest stop. Once inside, she automatically headed for the bathroom door when Jon grabbed her shoulder.

"Dude! Where are you going?"

She turned to look at him. "What?" The bathroom was right there.

"That's the women's room."

"Uh," Violet's stomach twisted and a cold sweat broke out. *Please don't let him notice*, she thought to herself. Then she looked at the door again. "So it is." She palmed her face. "Thanks, man. Told ya you were more awake than me." Then she followed him into the men's room.

How awkward.

Violet shouldn't be in here. But there was a first time for everything. Jon stood at the urinal along the wall, and she made a beeline to one of the stalls.

"You're awful private, Victor."

She said the first thing that came to mind. "Yeah, perks of growing up with an older sister." Callum was actually younger than her.

Jon chuckled. "No worries. See you by the soda machine."

"Yep."

Violet wiped the sweat from her forehead as she relieved herself. Dear God, that was close. She was so used to the environment inside NT that she hadn't remembered about the separate bathrooms. And that she shouldn't use the one for her actual gender.

She hurried as quickly as she could. Thank God he'd bought her line about the older sister. After washing her hands, she dabbed cold water on her eyes and wrists, hoping to wake herself up. Once she made it out of this assignment, she was never going undercover as a guy again. If she made it out of this in one piece, that was.

She made a big deal out of buying something with caffeine, and when she offered to take a turn driving, Jon turned her down, saying he didn't think she was awake enough. Violet shrugged off his good-natured ribbing. It felt like they'd broken through a wall of some kind.

After another hour or two on the road, she'd almost forgotten why they were on this trip.

They stopped for lunch around noon, grabbing take out after using the facilities. And this time, she remembered to use the men's room. Violet opted for the chicken strips, since they were easier to eat while driving and she'd insisted on giving Jon a break. He got a greasy burger, which he ate in the passenger seat while they discussed the differences between McDonald's and Burger King. Neither had a strong opinion, but Violet liked the fries better at McDonald's.

"Honestly, if I'm getting fast food, I'd rather go to Checker's."

Violet laughed. "I don't think I've ever seen one of those."

Jon grinned. "I grew up in Baltimore. You'll have to come check it out sometime. I'll make a convert out of you, Vic."

"If you say so." More like when pigs flew. She couldn't forget she was playing a part. "How much further until we get to this boat?"

"Take the next exit," responded the creepy automated voice from the GPS. They both chuckled at the appropriate timing.

Violet followed the voice's directions and drove them into a small harbor. There, they walked up to the harbor master's office where the keys were waiting for them. The harbor master was an older guy, with a gray mustache, and he led them down to the slip where a forty-foot trawler bobbed in the water. It had certainly seen better days. Violet was impressed with the way designers had used the space in what was obviously once a fishing vessel turned pleasure ship. A banquette and kitchenette filled the first floor of the boat, while the second floor below held a king-size bed and a small but functional bathroom, separated from the mechanical stuff by a wall.

"Let's get dinner." Jon said as the harbormaster left them on the boat unfortunately named *Riding U Dry*.

"Norm doesn't expect us back until tomorrow. I have no desire to be cooped up again this soon."

"I'm with you." Violet had to agree. "Although at least we can walk around and use a bathroom while we're on the water."

"True. But I'd like to savor our freedom before we go back."

"You won't hear me complain."

They drove over to a hole-in-the-wall restaurant named Fish Heads on the other end of the harbor boasting fresh fish. Violet got the grilled fish tacos while Jon killed some fish and chips.

"We should get going soon. I don't want to be too late getting back." Jon sipped at his soda through a straw.

Getting back. Violet didn't really want to go back. Even though she was playing a role, it felt as though all the syndicate shit had fallen to the wayside and they'd been able to just *be*. She gritted her teeth. She'd be on the clock until this was over, and she'd found a way out of NT's grasp.

Jon drove the van back to the end of the harbor *Riding U Dry* sat in. He left the key on the wheel like Norm had instructed, then they carried their bags onto the boat just as the sun was starting to set.

Exhaustion hit Violet as soon as they were down below. "I'm beat." She tossed her bag on the dresser squeezed next to the bed. "Are you okay taking the first shift driving?"

"Yeah, I got you. I'll wake you when I need a break." Jon dumped his bag on the floor and rooted through it for the coordinates Norm had given him for the warehouse back in Virginia.

Her beard itched. She needed a break. "I can set an alarm on my watch." She'd need time to reapply her beard before he saw her. Then she grabbed a towel out of her bag. "We can switch off."

"Sounds good." Jon headed up the stairs while she headed into the bathroom.

It took time to figure out how to maneuver around the small space, but Violet did it. The water was tepid at best.

Then just as she pulled the fake beard off, the boat started to move. Her whole body lurched to the side before she managed to catch herself with the handle on the shower wall. Someone obviously knew what they were doing when they put that there. Her toupee slipped from her hand and flew toward the toilet! She gasped and nearly faceplanted as she leaned forward to catch it while the boat was in motion. Grabbing it out of the air by the tips of her fingers, she leaned against the wall, hanging onto the handle for dear life while pressing the main component of her disguise against her heaving chest.

Shit, that had been a close call. Without that fake beard, she'd never pass as a man. She couldn't just grow a new one like someone with actual testosterone. But she couldn't linger long enough for her heart to stop racing. She had to get this thing dried out while Jon was busy driving and reapply before he saw her without it. Her cover would be completely blown and she'd be dead if she was lucky.

After wrapping herself in a towel, she cleaned the remains of the wig glue off her poor abused chin with Vaseline. She needed to let her skin rest. When she'd come up with this crazy scheme, she'd been thinking she could go back to that studio apartment she'd planned to rent and take the costume off every night. But Norm had dashed that plan.

It wasn't just the early morning getting to her today. Violet had been pretending twenty-four seven for weeks. She was *over* it.

If only she could reach out to Wanda. Her editor and mentor had to be losing her shit.

Violet emerged from the bathroom and headed for her bag. But a blinking light caught her eye on the floor opposite the dresser. Jon's phone!

He'd left his phone inside the bag when she left the room, probably hoping she wouldn't see it. But he must have had a message come through because the blue notification light was glowing, lighting up the dark inside of the bag.

This was her chance!

Violet stepped forward and grabbed the device, waking it up with a tap of her fingers. Fuck, of course it was password protected. Now what would Jon think was an easy number to remember?

She tried 1234, 0000, even 8675309. Nothing worked. And then the phone locked her out. It'd be ten minutes before his phone would allow her to try again. "Ugh!"

Then Violet and the phone went flying as Jon tackled her to the ground.

Chapter 11

Jon whistled as he set the coordinates into the navigation software in the bridge. He'd been trapped behind a desk in Annapolis for ages, and he'd missed the ocean. Even though this trawler was smaller than the ships he'd served on, the ocean was the same.

The Atlantic had been his home for many years, first on a submarine, and then on a carrier. He much preferred the floating city to the tin can. But he'd come back to dry land when he'd taken the desk job in Annapolis, wanting to be closer to his family. It'd been a long time.

He started humming "Brandy" as he untied the boat from the slip then bumped her out, putting her in reverse and back to neutral several times. Once he was past the slip, it was a short distance to the fairway. This boat had been kept on the end slip, probably due to its size. He didn't have to worry as much about the wind yet, not until they got out to the open ocean.

Damn, this boat was a beauty. He hated to think about what the syndicate was going to use it for.

With Victor in the shower two floors away, now was the perfect time to call Roger and give him an update. Jon reached into his pocket, but he didn't find his phone. Shit. He patted the other pocket. Damn it! Sticking both hands into his hoodie pocket, Jon realized he must have left the phone downstairs. Fuck.

He managed to get far enough away from the harbor that he didn't think they'd be in the way. Then he cut the engine, set the anchor and flipped the masthead light on. It was too close to evening to risk sitting on the edge of the ocean without a light on.

Jon didn't want to alert Victor that he'd left his phone within easy reach, so he tiptoed down the stairs on silent feet.

When he got to the lowest level, Victor stood there, freshly shaved and showered, holding his phone! Red tinged the edges of his vision. After everything, this guy had some balls to try and use his phone again! He didn't have time to think whether he'd deleted the messages to Roger. Jon just flew at him.

Victor gave a high-pitched shriek as Jon tackled him to the floor. He didn't care; he'd fucking *warned* the guy! His phone flew the opposite direction, but with the military-grade case he had on it, that was the least of his worries.

No, his focus was on his squirming roommate and nemesis underneath him on the floor of the ship. "I told you to stay away from my phone!"

The weasel kept trying to move his arms. "My... towel..."

"Ugh fine." Jon sat up, straddling Victor so he wouldn't escape. Victor immediately reached down and pulled the towel up over his tits.

His... tits?

"What the *fuck*?"

Jon took a second look at Victor's beardless face and realized what had been under his nose this entire time.

Victor was actually *Violet*!

He rubbed at his eyes in disbelief even as warmth spread through his chest. Relief swamped him. In fact, Jon was so shocked that he didn't see the slap coming until his head snapped so far to the side that it tipped his balance and Violet slipped from his grasp.

"Wait!" The door to the bathroom slammed shut.

The space wasn't that big. Jon could hear Violet thumping her head against the door as she let out a groan. "This isn't happening."

He jumped up, crossed the room in two steps and banged on the bathroom door. "Ra-no, you idiot," he muttered to himself. "Violet? It's me, Jon."

"I know who you are, fucker!"

Jon scrubbed a hand over his face. He was fucking this up. "I've been looking for you."

"That's not reassuring right now." She muttered something to herself that Jon didn't catch.

"Sweetheart, please. I've been worried sick. Wanda said you missed your check ins." And the reason Victor wanted to use his phone made sense now. "Fuck, that's why you kept trying to steal my phone, isn't it?"

"I wasn't going to keep it!" She shrieked. Then she caught up to what else he'd said. "Wanda?"

"Wanda sent me. I'm not going to tell on you, baby. You're safe." He scrubbed a hand through his hair. This was getting them nowhere. "I'm going back upstairs so you can get dressed. Then we need to talk. Come find me when you're done, Mona—I mean Violet." He refused to say "ready" because Lord knew *he* wasn't ready to discuss the last four years. But they were going to do it, anyway. He hoped.

Jon grabbed his phone from where it had fallen and trudged up to the galley. Roger had forwarded him a funny meme from Nadia about mothers of the bride. He added a laughing reaction. Poor thing. Judy Hunt was driving his sister nuts trying to control her wedding, and frankly Jon was starting to think marriage was a bad idea if it made Mom crazy like this.

He shot off a message to Roger.

> **Jon: The package is safe, let the customer know we have it in hand.**

It was late and Roger might be asleep, but he'd get back to him eventually. Then he reached into the mini fridge and grabbed two bottles of water he'd brought along with them. He had energy drinks in there too, not planning to use them, but if he and Violet were up all night talking then he'd chug one to get them back to NT on time.

They needed to be on the same page before they returned. He sat down facing the stairs, focusing on his breathing so his adrenaline would calm down.

Soft footfalls heralded Violet's entrance. Now that he'd seen her for who she was, he didn't understand how he could have missed it. Large, loose clothes hid her figure, but her face was clearly Violet.

"How'd you get the beard to look so real?" He blurted out before realizing it. Damn, maybe he needed that caffeine just for this conversation.

"It's a toupee for your chin, basically. And I use a lot of wig glue." She slid onto the other side of the banquette, folding her hands together. "What are you doing here?"

He hated the distance, but he didn't want to push her. "Wanda hired my brother Roger's company to extract you when you missed your check-ins. I was the best option to come get you. And when she showed us your picture and explained what your job is, I wanted to come because suddenly a lot of things made sense." He raised both eyebrows and tilted his head. Jon pushed one of the water bottles at her before snagging his own.

She cracked the seal and took a sip. "That means you're not... you didn't look all that surprised when you got here."

"I knew what I was getting into," he explained. "My brothers' girls have had dealings with the syndicate before. They actually rescued someone from a syndicate facility. So, I knew going in what I was dealing with."

"I don't understand. How did Wanda find you?"

"Her brother was Roger's CO in the Army. She reached out at his recommendation."

She tilted her head and furrowed her brow. "This is not a normal Army-type mission."

Jon shrugged. "He was Special Forces. For him, it kind of is. Only he couldn't do the actual undercover bit because the syndicate already knows his face. That's part of why I came."

"What's the other part?" She eyed him warily.

He closed the water bottle and slid onto her side of the table, the anger at her disappearance starting to rise again. "Because we have unfinished business." She tried to move away but couldn't get very far in the small space. Up close, he watched as her pupils dilated. "What the actual *fuck*, Ramona? Where the hell have you been?"

He cupped her face in both hands, careful of her chin where she must have spread something to heal her battered skin. "You really suffer for your art, don't you?"

"It's my dream job." Her voice had lost the deeper, hard quality she affected with Victor. Now she sounded like a woman. Like his Ramona.

"I came to see you that night. You were gone. You disconnected your *phone*." He couldn't keep the frustration and anger out of his voice. Her eyes closed tightly, as though the memory pained her.

"I had to."

"No, you didn't." He ran his fingers over her soft, short hair. Jon couldn't believe he'd finally found her again after all this time. And right under his nose, dressed as a guy.

Ramona —damn it, *Violet* — licked her lips. "I never thought I'd see you again."

"Clearly." He took a sip of his water to quench his dry throat and give him a moment to get a handle on his composure.

"I hated lying to you."

His water bottle hit the table with a thunk. "You couldn't have let me in on the secret?"

She shook her head. "It would have compromised the story."

"I felt like an idiot." He remembered showing up with a bouquet of flowers to ask her to be his girlfriend and finding an empty apartment. "I thought you felt something, and then you completely ghosted me."

"I... I did feel something. That's why..." She looked away, tilting her face down. "That's why I had to go."

"You couldn't look me up after? I would have understood."

She shook her head. "That's not how it works."

Jon sighed. It was clear she wasn't going to give in on this. He hadn't been important enough for her to let him in, or to find him afterward. His heart sank at the reminder that he was only ever wanted for a good time, not a long time.

He tried to get them back to business. They each had a job to do. "I let Roger know that I found you, and to tell Wanda you're okay."

Violet released a breath, and he swore she looked like a twenty-pound weight had been lifted off her. "Thank you. I'm sure she's been worried."

"I believe the word she used was terrified." He licked his lips. "We all were. Knowing what my brother's girl went through at their hands, we all assumed the worst; that they'd discovered you and shipped you off."

Violet shook her head. "No, the last time I spoke with Wanda, I had gone up to the roof. It was during a big thunderstorm. Right after we hung up, I got one of those emergency alerts in my ear. It made me jump, then my phone slipped out of my hand and off the roof."

"Damn." He sat back and stared at her. "Why do they always wait until the storm is right on top of you to send those things?"

She gave a relieved giggle, sounding like his Ramona again. It brought back that familiar warm feeling he used to get thinking about her. "I know, right? I don't need a warning; I'm literally standing in it right now!"

The hilarity of the situation finally hit them and they both dissolved into laughter.

"So, you kept trying to steal my phone so you could reach out to Wanda. Why didn't you just tell me who you are?"

"I thought you were here willingly, as part of them."

Jon made a sound of pure horror and his jaw dropped. "Seriously? Do you think that little of me?"

Violet shrugged. "It's been four years. How was I supposed to know? And we didn't exactly get to know each other much outside the bedroom back then."

"Because you were undercover." His voice flattened, but she didn't seem to notice.

"Yes. It's highly effective for getting information people don't want to give me." She took another sip of her water.

"Is it ethical, though?"

"It worked for Nellie Bly. And I don't particularly care about ethics when I'm exposing criminal activity. If they were worried about ethics, I wouldn't be there in the first place."

"Fair point." Jon carefully considered his next thought, then internally said, "fuck it." If he was going to get another shot with her, he'd have to take her as she was. At least this time she wasn't hiding who she was from him. "Is it a good idea to tell you how hot I think it all is?"

She blinked rapidly, her brown eyes wide. "What?"

"While I was waiting to infiltrate the syndicate, I read all your articles online. You're incredible."

A pink flush covered her cheeks. "T-thank you."

Beautiful, intelligent, and a bad ass. Jon was positive now that his crush from four years ago was back in full force, despite her deceit. Her tongue darted out to moisten her lips, and he followed it with his gaze.

"I missed you." He blurted out.

She averted her gaze. "You didn't know me."

"Are you sure about that?" He reached out and traced her ear with his thumb, remembering how he used to tuck her long strands back from her face. "Were you acting when it was just us?"

She bit at her lip. Jon wanted to tug it out from under her teeth but he stayed perfectly still. Normally he had no problems chasing a woman but, in this instance, it would be best for her to come to him. "Not entirely. Once I figured out you had nothing to do with the backroom deals, I was as real with you as I dare be."

"Just not with your name or your real profession."

Her gaze dropped to the table. "I have a brother."

That's right. Ramona had always said she was an only child. "You were protecting him."

"Of course. I couldn't be sure who else listened in when we were at the bar."

It made sense, and he hated it. Looking down at her, her innocent brown eyes captured him as they had that night so long ago. God, it was hard to remember this was the woman who'd lied to his face. Who'd left him without a warning or explanation. He had to keep that in mind or this was going to go sideways. But still, he had to be sure.

"You said you felt it, too. What we had was real."

The blush on her face deepened and Violet shook her head. "It... it couldn't be."

Hope bloomed in his chest as Jon cupped her cheek, turning her back to face him, and stared into her eyes. "Then kiss me and let's find out."

Her gaze dropped to his mouth, then lifted back to his eyes. Jon's heartbeat sounded like a Riverdance performance in his ears as he waited for her to accept his challenge. She lifted her arms and laid them loosely around his shoulders. Then she slowly pulled on the back of his neck, and his lips tingled as she brought him down to her mouth.

Their lips met and sparks ignited. It'd been four years since Jon felt this pure electricity, four years of increasingly fewer lackluster hookups, and when he took control of the kiss, wrapping one arm around her waist and hauling her nearly into his lap, he knew she felt it too. The way she moaned and melted into his embrace, her lithe fingers gripping the short hairs at the back of his head. Four years of longing, of loneliness, erupted between them.

She was what he'd been missing all this time. And he was never going to let her go.

Chapter 12

Violet's nerve endings lit up like the fourth of July as she lost herself in Jon's kiss. He'd taken the lead after she started it, a delightful change for someone accustomed to frequent decision-making. Especially when the person taking charge was someone who knew the female body the way Jonathon Hunt did.

His tongue explored her mouth with gentle strokes as his hand grabbed a handful of her ass and gripped her tight. The opposing sensations made Violet groan against his mouth as she ground her center against his thigh. The wooden table behind her was bolted to the floor, however, so she couldn't actually straddle his lap like she wanted.

Reluctantly she broke the kiss, but he didn't let her go far, breathing her air like her mouth was his oxygen mask.

"We... should move," she gasped out.

He grinned, panting into her mouth. "Sounds good." Then her back was flat on the table, Jon leaning over her, kissing her once more. "Wanna see you." His hands slid under her sweatshirt as his lips traveled down her neck.

"Yes!" Her voice was quickly muffled by the fabric of her shirt as he pulled it over her head. His eager hands pulled her pants and underwear off just as fast, then he stopped and stared at her laid out like his own personal feast.

Thank God he remembered she liked a rougher touch. He pinched her nipples, and she bowed her back off the table, trying to get closer. There was something erotic about being naked before someone fully dressed, and Violet reveled in it. His shirt rubbing against her naked skin was electrifying as he bent and nipped, sucked and gently bit her breasts.

Her moans echoed throughout the cabin as he drove her higher and higher. When she was squirming with need, he finally lifted off her. But instead of pulling his clothes off like she expected, he gripped her hips and flipped her over onto her stomach.

"You've been a naughty girl, Violet. Disappearing on me like that. Making everyone worry about you being in danger." He leaned back over to whisper in her ear, his jeans rubbing against her ass. "I oughta spank you."

Violet whimpered as her pussy clenched.

"Do it."

Permission granted, Jon stood back up. Cool air hit her skin and she shivered, but not from the temperature. His hand gently stroked her cheeks at the edge of the table, where her legs hung over the edge, her toes barely scraping the floor.

Pain cracked across one ass cheek, and she cried out. Heat bloomed, and Jon immediately soothed the spot he'd struck. "Okay?"

She nodded, panting.

"Say red if you want me to stop."

Dear God, she'd missed this.

Jon rained smacks down across her ass and upper thighs, heat spreading until the pain turned into pleasure.

She floated on that feeling, losing count of the spanks until Jon decided she'd had enough. He soothed the burn with his hands, then cupped her mound.

"You're soaked," he murmured as he thrust two fingers inside her.

Violet arched her back and screamed, the orgasm taking them both by surprise.

"Damn, your pussy is squeezing my fingers so good. I can't wait to get my cock in you."

He brought her down from that high, then rolled her back over and lifted her into his arms. Which was good because her bones were jelly and her head was swimming.

Jon carried her down the stairs. "Our first time in four years is not going to be on a table." He laid her on the king size bed, then rummaged through his bag and tossed a foil packet next to her. Then he paused. "Do you want to?"

She didn't even care that he'd brought condoms. The sailor in him was probably always prepared. "Get naked and fuck me, Navy boy."

He smirked. "You know I was an officer, right?"

She propped herself up on her elbows. "What? What were you doing at the Rusty Nail?"

"Avoiding the uniform chasers." He lifted his shirt and Violet whistled. Firm pecs and washboard abs covered with a dusting of hair that ended in a line leading straight to his zipper. It had been a long four years. Then he undid his belt as she watched and unzipped his jeans, letting them fall to the floor. His cock tented his black boxer briefs, and Violet moaned.

"Last chance to back out."

"Hell no."

Jon dropped his boxers, and his erection bounced up, pointing straight at her like a dowsing rod. He crawled on the bed and she reached for him, but he pushed her hand away.

"If you touch me, I'm going to go off like a rocket and that's way too soon." He ripped open the foil packet and rolled the condom over his dick, then lifted her legs over his shoulders. "I wanna be so deep in you, you'll never get rid of me."

"Yessssss," she moaned as he slid in, her channel welcoming him home, ignoring the implication that he would stick with her. They groaned in unison as he bottomed out, Violet feeling so full at this angle. He rose on his knees, holding her thighs to his chest, and gave a slow thrust.

Oh fuck! He was like a homing missile to her G-spot. Fuck, she'd missed this. The few one-night stands she'd had never measured up to her memories. After a while she'd started to think she'd exaggerated them in her mind. Violet was glad to know she hadn't. "Oh my God, right there!"

Sweat beaded on his forehead as he gave a few more teasing thrusts, then he shuddered. "This isn't going to take long, sweetheart."

"I'm right there with you."

Her confession must have given him the permission he needed, because next thing she knew, he was pounding into her G-spot like a beast unleashed. "Oh, fuck. Violet. Vee. Baby," he chanted over and over like a prayer.

"Ahhh!" she cried out as the orgasm hit her like a freight train, her back arching, legs spasming, pussy clenching around his cock like a vise. She pulled him over the edge, his groan echoing in the enclosed space as his hips stuttered.

He caught himself above her on his hands, panting, sweat dripping down his nose. They stayed locked in that moment while they caught their breath, then Jon slipped from her and fell down on his side. "Holy shit."

"Yeah." Violet wasn't sure she'd ever recover. "Was it that good before...?"

Jon shook his head. "No. Not even close. God *damn*, baby." He stood on shaky legs to dispose of the condom, then crawled back into bed with her, pulling her into his arms. She was still liquid, but she wouldn't have put up any resistance even if she wasn't. She'd missed this so damn much.

But as they lay there basking in the afterglow, her brain started to come back online. Ignoring the fact that this was just another short-term fling, the syndicate was front and center. "Tell me what I got myself into."

Jon sighed and pushed his hair back over his head. "The syndicate is a nationwide, possibly international, organized crime ring. We know they have their hands in jewelry theft, hacking, and human trafficking. My brother runs Hunt Security, and he stumbled upon it thanks to a job, and now they're working with the FBI to get it taken down."

Her thoughts flitted to that list of names she'd recognized and she internally smacked her forehead. She'd been right. "Why not send the FBI in?"

"First, Wanda called *us*. And Sam, who used to work for them, knows all about the red tape they'd have to wade through to get to you. It was better to just go in and try to find you ourselves."

"You'd rather ask for forgiveness than permission."

Jon grinned. "That's my brother."

"But you were in the Navy... what happened?"

Jon shrugged. "Got sick of the bureaucracy myself, and I wanted to spend more time at home with my family."

She nodded. "You never told me you were an officer."

He smirked. "A lot of women hear 'officer' and think 'sugar daddy.' Not the type of person I want to be with."

"Fair," she said as she snuggled in closer. "Instead, you ended up with someone who didn't exist."

"Found you anyway," he said with a smirk. "Don't get between a Hunt and his partner."

She snorted. "Kinda funny hearing a guy like you say 'partner' and not 'woman'."

Now it was his turn to snort. "Trust me, we learned our lesson when we tried to get between my baby sister and her man. It doesn't matter the gender."

Violet laughed. She remembered his stories about Nadia. That girl had always struck her as quite the spitfire.

"You know, you were really good at pretending you didn't know anything about me or my family. You had me completely fooled."

She bit back the rest of her laughter. "It wasn't easy. And I hated that you had gotten involved with these guys." She shuddered, remembering their initiation. "Back there at NT, in those rooms... did you actually..."

"Fuck her? Hell no." Thunder clouded his face. "Whatever you thought of me, don't ever think I'd get hard in a situation like *that*." He spat out the last word.

"I'm sorry, it's just... I'm having a difficult time wrapping my brain around what's going on here."

He tapped her on the nose. "What's going on is I was undercover to find you. And now I can get you out."

She bolted upright. "But my story's not done! I need more time, Jon."

"Mo—Violet, it's too dangerous. We have to find a way to extricate you from these guys."

"Not until I have enough for my article. I'm taking them down." She slid backward, away from him. How could she have let this happen again? "I've barely scratched the surface. It took me ages to get them to trust me." He furrowed his brow, and conflict shone in his mossy green eyes, showing her the way out of this mess. "Please, help me keep the disguise going. I need more information."

His resigned sigh told her his answer. "Of course, I'll help with your ruse. You'd be in too much danger if I didn't. But we need to get out as soon as there's an opening." He sat up and cupped her cheek with one hand. "I can't lose you again."

"I'm not going anywhere," she swore, sticking to her guns. "We'll have to be careful, though. They'll bug this boat once they get their paws on it. I know because I've heard Norm tell them to install the microphones before." That phone Norm gave her was probably bugged as well. Good thing she hadn't turned it on.

"Right. At least we're roommates." He smirked.

She shook her head vehemently, her eyes wide. "Are you crazy? Those walls are thin as hell. We don't dare."

"That's not going to work for me then, because I won't be able to keep my hands off you."

"You'd better, or we'll both get caught!" Good grief, did he have a death wish?

Jon sighed. "Alright. But when this is all over, I'm coming for you, Violet Giordano." He checked his watch. "I better get up there and get this boat moving. We've got about a twelve-hour trip back and we're too close to the harbor for my liking."

"You wore me out, lover boy. I'm going to nap and then I'll come up and spell you, okay?"

"I look forward to it, sweetheart." He leaned in and kissed her sweetly on the mouth. She sighed and pulled away.

"That was your last one."

He pouted. "Then we need to get this job done ASAP." Jon lifted himself off the bed, and she mourned the loss of his arms. She watched him bend over and wished things were different as she caught sight of his perfectly round butt. Damn, she wanted to bite it. Violet nearly whimpered as he pulled the rest of his clothes on. "Get some rest. I'll be up on the bridge."

"Is it called a bridge when the boat is this small?"

"It's always the bridge, baby. Now sleep so I can get my job done and my girl back."

As Violet curled up under the covers, she had the fleeting thought that the idea of being his girl sounded awful nice.

Nope, no way. She couldn't be his girl. Relationships and a successful career like hers didn't mix. Thinking back to what Wanda had told her just before she went undercover about Mark, she buried her face in the pillows. He had to choose between his career and his personal life.

She'd already chosen her career. She couldn't have that and Jon, too.

Chapter 13

Violet woke up feeling refreshed. She left her beard on the dresser, since it was still drying out, and got dressed. When she emerged from the staircase onto the bridge, Jon was sitting at the helm, looking out at the ocean filled with stars.

"Wow," she breathed. The cabin was dark with just the light of the instruments glowing, lighting him up like an extraterrestrial.

"Stunning, isn't she? I've missed the ocean."

She wandered up to stand by his side. "I've never seen so many stars."

Jon cut the engine and turned out all the lights. The moon shone in the water like a mirror, and the stars reflecting in the sea made the sky look endless.

All her concerns, her fears, fell away as she stared. Somehow, she felt both infinite and small, as she gazed out into eternity. "That's incredible."

"It puts everything into perspective." Jon spoke in a hush, like they were in a church. And it did feel holy. Something most humans would never get to experience. "We're so tiny in the grand scheme of things. Humans could fall off the face of the Earth and she would still be here. The ocean goes on, no matter what we do to it."

Violet's gaze dropped to the where the waves danced around their boat. "Why are humans so awful to everything? Even each other?"

Jon chuckled. "A line from Mary Poppins just popped into my head. She talked about people who can't see past the end of their nose. I think most people can't see the bigger picture. That we're all part of the same family. The same home."

Violet's eyes prickled, and she blinked rapidly. "It's so sad. What we do to each other."

"Yeah, it is. But we do what we can to fix it." She felt his gaze turn to her. "Like you, with your writing. You're changing the world."

Violet shook her head, even though she knew he couldn't see her in the dark. "I can't change the whole world. One piece of it, maybe."

"You took a drug ring off the streets. You've exposed corrupt police departments and caused cities to clean house. You're doing so much and you don't even realize it, Violet. And I have no doubts you're going to keep doing this for as long as you can. Your legacy is going to be incredible."

Her cheeks heated, and Violet was grateful for the darkness. "How about you turn the lights back on and show me how to drive this thing? I don't want to take too long and give Norm a reason to suspect us of anything."

Jon chuckled, like he knew the real reason she was changing the subject, and did as she requested. He gave her a quick run-down of how to read the navigation and how to keep them on course, as well as what to do if she saw another ship out there. They could still see the coastline so he wasn't expecting them to run into anything like a cruise ship, but she felt relatively confident she could do this.

"And if there's a problem, yell for me. I'll leave the door open so I can hear you."

"Aye, aye, Captain." She gave him a jaunty salute.

Jon shook his head. "I was only a Lieutenant, Vee. Not a Captain." He hesitated, then leaned in and kissed her forehead. She pulled back reluctantly.

"Jon..."

He pursed his lips. "Give me until we see the warehouse, please? Just let me pretend it's you and me on a joyride, not bringing this gorgeous boat back to a bunch of criminals."

She sighed. "I don't want to get used to it."

His shoulders slumped forward. "I understand. No more until we're free." He squeezed her arm once, then made his way down the stairs. "I mean it. Call me for anything," he called up.

"Night, Jon." Resigned, she settled down in the captain's chair and took over driving for the night.

Left alone with nothing but her thoughts for company, Violet's mind drifted back four years ago, when she'd first met Jon.

She'd worn her sexiest tank top and skinny jeans with high heels. Standing at the bar waiting for the bartender to fucking notice her already, so she could get this order to her table, she sensed a presence behind her, and spun around to spy a tall man whose black t-shirt barely contained his muscles, with a short military style haircut and green eyes that sparkled when he caught sight of her.

"Hello there," she said, her charm turned up to eleven as she leaned back against the bar. Could he be a bouncer? Or maybe someone else who worked here that she could pump for information? She'd only been working there for two weeks and didn't know everyone yet.

"Can I buy you a drink?"

She had to give him credit; he didn't look away from her face. "Sorry, honey, I'm working."

Violet winced as she remembered how much they used to hang out at the Rusty Nail specifically so she could get intel for her story. Once she'd understood he had nothing to do with the drugs, she'd kept seeing him under false pretenses.

Why, though? What was it about Jon that drew her in? She'd never gotten this close to anyone else while she was undercover. That was the rule her college mentor, Carol, taught her. *"You can't be memorable when you're undercover. Your job is to blend into the woodwork."*

Investigative journalism was her first love. She'd dreamed of this since she was a little girl. But relationships got in the way, as she learned when she was around eight years old. Her mom had had hopes and dreams, but because of her marriage, she hadn't been able to follow them. Violet could still recall that awkward dinner.

"Now that the kids are both in school, I was thinking about picking up classes again," Mom said to Dad as she ladled mashed potatoes from a bowl. "The community college has the perfect schedule."

"You don't need to go back to school. That's why I work. I provide and you stay home with the kids."

"But the kids are at school all day. There's no reason I can't do both."

"What happens if one of them gets sick? I can't take time off."

Back and forth, Mom argued with Dad until finally Dad had enough. "No, and that's the end of it. I'm not paying for your college."

Violet never did learn what her mom wanted to do with her life. Her father was killed on the job several years later, a beam falling at the construction site, prompting her mom to try to find work wherever she could.

She waited tables while Violet's neighbor came over and watched them after school. Then when Violet was old enough for a house key, she would cook all day on her days off so that Violet could heat something up for her and Callum's dinner. Around the time Violet was eighteen, her mother urged her to go to college, not work as she'd intended.

"This is your future, Violet," she'd said. "You need a college degree to get by in this world."

"You get by just fine," she'd argued. "I can find a job and still write on the side."

Mom just shook her head. God, she'd been so tired, Violet didn't understand how she hadn't seen the diagnosis coming. "You're both going to college."

Halfway through her bachelor's, the doctors diagnosed Mom with cancer. Stage three. Callum had just started school half a state away, and Violet was at NYU pursuing her dream. Mom's sister had come to stay with her and help her through treatment, and when they arrived for winter break, they'd been shocked.

"What's going on, Aunt Shirley?" Violet dropped her suitcase in the small foyer and unwrapped her scarf.

"Oh good, you're here." Aunt Shirley wiped her hands on Mom's apron. "Your brother wasn't happy we wanted to wait, but I don't want your mom to have to explain things twice."

"What are you talking about?" Violet shucked her coat and tossed it on its hook, then followed her into the den.

The small TV room that had been there all Violet's life had been turned into a bedroom. Mom lay in the small bed, propped up with pillows, a silver IV stand glinting next to her. Her raven locks were gone; her head covered in a scarf.

Her face was pale and drawn, but she smiled and reached for Violet. "Welcome home, dear."

Callum sat next to Mom in a chair, leaning his elbows on his knees, trying to keep his leg from bouncing. He wasn't successful. Their eyes met as Violet reached over the bed to hug her mom. His were wide with fear and uncertainty. All Violet felt was confused.

Then Mom explained her diagnosis. The doctors said she didn't have much time left. Violet and Callum both wanted to quit school, but Mom wouldn't hear of it.

"Don't give up your dreams for anyone. Promise me." Of course, they promised. How could they not?

Violet wiped a stray tear from her cheek. It had been ages since she thought of that awful day. Mom died six months later, and she and Callum had agreed to sell the house to pay what they could of the medical bills and their student debt. Callum lived in New York City now, living out his fashion design and drag dreams. She'd moved to Gainesville, Virginia outside DC to work at InVestigate. They usually talked on a regular basis, but she'd told him she was going undercover and would be out of contact. She hadn't wanted him to worry, since they were all the other had left.

No matter how good Jon was in bed, she couldn't let this chemistry derail her plans. Most of the married people she worked with either had lackluster careers or strained relationships with their spouses. She'd seen no fewer than five divorces in the office since she'd started, usually because the spouse felt like her colleague put the job first instead of them. Wanda only had pictures of her nieces and nephews on her desk. She'd never worn a ring and Violet had never asked. Everything that Violet had seen had told her falling in love would hold her back. And her career was too important to mess up for a boyfriend.

It didn't matter how amazing Jon was for coming after her. She'd have to let him go again regardless.

Jon tossed and turned, but he couldn't shut his mind off enough to sleep. Sex with Violet had blown his mind. She should be down here, in his arms, not driving the boat back to their prison.

They had the ownership paperwork onboard. They could just sail away, and disappear from the syndicate.

As tempting an idea as that was, he knew Violet would shoot him down. She wanted her story, and frankly he wanted to make sure she got it. But if she was discovered, they'd both need to flee. He wouldn't let them hurt her.

He looked at his phone and debated calling Finn. It was midnight in Arizona, where he and Josie were on their road trip. Jon sent a text first.

Jon: You up?

Finn: Yeah why?

Jon: Can I call?

Jon's phone rang in his hand. "Hey," he answered.

"Hey." Finn's hushed voice came over the line. "One sec while I step outside."

A door opened and closed and then Finn spoke normally. "Josie fell asleep after hiking the Grand Canyon with me, and I don't want to wake her."

"Did you have fun?"

"Yeah, it was awesome." He could hear the grin in Finn's voice. "But I don't think that's why you called.""I wanted to let you know I found Violet. She's okay."

His little brother let out a hushed whoop. "Oh, thank God! Where did you find her?"

Jon chuckled. "Little minx was dressed as a dude. We've been roommates this whole time and I had no idea."

"Wow. Those are some next-level skills." Finn paused. "So, when are you going home?"

"It's not that simple. I'd disappear on them right now but she wants to finish her story."

"How would you do that?" Finn sounded thoughtful.

"It'd be perfect. They assigned us to go pick up a boat in Charleston and bring it back to the warehouse. We're in the Atlantic sailing back tonight. But she's not ready to come home and I don't want to leave her alone. In fact, I'm supposed to be sleeping since I drove the last four hours, but I can't."

"Why not?"

Jon scrubbed a hand over his face. "We... I..."

"You fucked, didn't you?"

He groaned just thinking about it. "Maybe."

Finn snorted. "Ain't no maybe about it. So, what's there to think about?"

"I want her for more than one night, but we can't let the syndicate know about it. It's too dangerous."

Silence filled the air so long Jon had to check his phone to make sure the call hadn't dropped. It was definitely possible out here on the ocean. But no, it was still connected.

"I think you're smart to wait. The syndicate is no joke, and you don't want to risk them discovering who she really is. But that doesn't mean you can't pick up where you left off once this is done. Just make sure she gets what she needs, then get her out of there."

That made sense. It was essentially what he'd decided upstairs, but it helped having someone else affirm his plan. "Yeah, I think that's what I'm going to do."

An idea came to mind, one that might get Violet out of danger that much sooner. "Do you think Josie would talk to her?"

"I'll ask her tomorrow. As long as she protected Josie's name, I think she'd agree."

"She changed the names in all of her other articles, so I doubt it'll be a problem." Jon yawned, his mind finally catching up to his body. "I'll see you when we're both back, Finn."

"Stay safe, brother. And keep her safe, too."

"Same to you. See you soon."

Jon hung up the phone and relaxed into the mattress as sleep finally took him.

Chapter 14

J ON REENTERED THE BRIDGE as dawn broke across the sky.

"Good morning," Violet called from the helm. "Sleep well?"

"Well enough," he answered, bringing two cups of coffee with him. He'd doctored one the way he remembered Violet took it four years ago, hoping that was still the case.

"Thanks." She accepted the cup and took a sip, then looked at him in shock. "You remembered!"

"Of course." He settled into the co-captain's chair, sipping at his own mug of liquid gold as he consulted the navigation software. "We should be there by lunchtime. Did you want to get some more sleep?"

"Nah, I'll take a nap when we get there."

They talked about everything and nothing. It turned out Violet actually had a younger brother, but his drag persona's name was Anita Dik. Jon snorted at the name. "What is he, twelve?"

"Oh, all their names are like that. Sexual innuendo and pun city." She took another sip of her coffee. "They're amazing and I love it. I always make time to see a show when I go to visit."

"Do you visit often?"

"It depends on my work schedule. He works for himself so he's flexible but if I have time between projects I go stay for the weekend." She bit at her lip, her nerves evident. "He's all I've got left since Mom died."

"I'm sorry." His heart squeezed in his chest. Jon couldn't imagine life without his parents around. "Your dad?"

"Died when I was a kid." She looked over the instruments. "How's your family?"

"Well, Nadia is getting married, and my mom is driving her crazy. Her fiancé is Caleb, and he drives a motorcycle and does LARP with us. I wasn't too sure about him, but he's perfect for her. Roger and Finn have both paired off.

Roger fell in love with a girl he was guarding, and Finn..." He took a deep breath. He hadn't talked to anyone about this since his family had all experienced the same thing. "Finn was the only surviving member of his Marine squad after they ran over an IED, and he lost his arm."

"Holy shit. The sniper?" Violet's eyes were saucers.

"Yeah. Finn came home but he wasn't taking care of himself. So Roger asked a nursing student he was guarding at the time to help him out. Not only did she whip him into shape, they fell in love."

"Wow. That's amazing."

Jon let the smile lift one side of his mouth. "Yeah, it was quite the love story. Mom is glad we're all home. But I'm pretty sure we're not telling her about the dangerous security work Roger's got us taking on because she'll just worry again like she used to. She wasn't handling Finn's last deployment very well, and then he got hurt."

"I'm sorry about his arm, but I'm glad he survived."

"Me, too." Jon blinked rapidly, unwilling to cry when his family had been the lucky ones.

About an hour out from their destination, Jon turned to her. "I hate to say this, but you should probably go put your beard on."

"You're right. It's been nice having it off, though."

"We could just cut and run and you wouldn't have to put it on at all." He kept his tone light and joking, but he'd absolutely run if she was willing.

She glared at him, fists clenched on the arms of her chair. "No way. I'm not leaving without my story."

He shrugged. "It was worth a try." At the surprised look on her face, he sighed. "Look, I'm not going to force you to leave. I'm not here to kidnap you. I'm here to help. Just promise you won't let another opportunity like this go, okay? These people are dangerous." He waved her away from the controls. "Go handle your business, Vee. I'll take us in."

"Okay." She stood and let him take over her seat. "And Jon?" He looked up at her, pointedly not looking at her chest. "Thanks for coming after me." She pressed her lips to his forehead in a quick kiss then headed for the stairs.

"Anytime." He called out as she disappeared below deck. He'd follow her anywhere.

By the time Nautical Transit's warehouse appeared on the water, Violet was back up top with their bags and their trash, her fake beard perfectly in place. Victor. He had to think of Violet as Victor, like he would at a LARP event. That was all this was; live-action roleplay — with deadly stakes.

Violet/Victor showed him where to pull the boat into the warehouse and there were guys on the dock ready to tie them to the slip. He nodded at Jameson, the only other person whose name he remembered besides Victor and Norm.

"Good trip?" Jameson asked him.

"It was fine." Jon watched Violet dump the trash they'd taken from the boat so no one saw the used condom. Victor. Damn it. Now that he'd seen the truth, he couldn't unsee it.

"Norm's waiting for you in the office." Jameson clapped them both on the shoulder. "We'll take over from here."

Right. Bugging the boat. Jon gave him a stiff nod and followed Victor to Norm's office.

"Hey boss, we're back," Violet spoke in Victor's deeper tone, which helped convince Jon's brain of her character.

"Great!" Norm looked up from his computer screen and his gaze darted back and forth between them. "You boys getting along?"

"We got along just fine." Jon gave his most charming grin and slapped Violet on the back. "We're best buds now."

Violet was stiff as stone. Jon wasn't sure Norm was buying what he was trying to sell, but at least he seemed convinced there were no major problems.

"That's great to hear. I've decided to put the two of you on a pick-up assignment. Once the boys are done prepping the boat, you're going to go pick up some merchandise and bring it back here. I'll give you Jameson and Billy Bob for guard duty."

Jon's heart sank. "Sounds good, boss. I'm going to get some shuteye, I'm wiped."

"Yeah, me too," said Violet.

"Alright boys. I'll see you later."

They didn't speak until they got back to their dorm room on the fourth floor. Jon opened his mouth as soon as the door shut, but Violet put her finger to his lips and shook her head. She reached inside her bag and pulled out a strange device, then slowly passed it over every nook and cranny in the small room. After she finished sweeping the room, she nodded and put it back in her bag. "No bugs."

"Got it. Should have thought of that." She was smart not to trust these people as far as she could throw them. They were still the newest people here.

"I couldn't sweep it once you got here, but I did it every time I came back in the room after a shift." She shrugged. "Never found anything, but since we were gone so long I wanted to be sure." Violet threw herself onto her bed and sighed. "This is happening really fast."

"It sure seems that way." He lowered himself to his own mattress.

"It's like the moment they've decided to trust me, they throw everything at me."

Jon shrugged. "At least you're finally getting somewhere."

"True." She pulled her hoodie off and tossed it at the end of the bed. "We should get some sleep."

He kneeled at the edge of her bed so she could hear him whisper. "Shouldn't we plan our escape? Once you talk to the victims you'll have enough for your story, right?"

"I don't know." She scrubbed a hand over her face. "I'm not running on enough cylinders to think about it right now."

"Okay, Vee. Sleep well." Jon flipped the light out, then stripped down to his boxers. They might as well both sleep, though he'd rather be in bed with her. But there was barely room on the twin bed for one of them, let alone both. He double checked that he'd locked the door, laid down, and let exhaustion take him.

When they woke up for dinner, it was as though the previous night hadn't happened. Violet grunted at his "good evening" instead of good morning, and headed for the bathroom. Jon immediately threw clothes on and followed, concerned that she was going to be seen. But she used a stall, like she had when they stopped on the road.

That's when he remembered she almost went into the women's room, and he'd had to stop her. He splashed cold water on his face. How had he not seen it?

He walked down to dinner with her, where a group of the guys were playing cards over their meatloaf. Jon grabbed a tray and piled a plate with food. Violet followed after him with her own tray.

There was only one seat open at the poker table, so Jon looked to Violet. But she had started toward an empty table. When he went to follow her, she glared back at him and shook her head subtly. Alright, then. He slid into the empty chair with the guys playing poker. Jameson looked up from his hand.

"Shall we deal you in next hand?"

"Nah, man. I'm good."

He ate in silence, listening to the men bluff and harass each other around him. How could they be so normal about all of this? It felt weird. He guessed not everyone had been raised with the same sense of honor he and his brothers had, and that simultaneously angered and saddened him. Jon thought about the other businesses Violet's articles had exposed, prompting investigations, and he knew the FBI was working on the syndicate as a whole.

Josie was a huge part of that investigation. But they were taking so long. How many victims would slip through the cracks because of it?

"Did you catch the name on that boat?" Billy Bob asked as he drew a card. "*Riding U Dry*. I wish we could keep it, 'cause it fits."

"You know the rules." Jameson shuffled the cards around. "The boats don't get names."

"But it's perfect! Most of those bitches are dry as hell when you fuck 'em."

Jon ground his back teeth, swallowing his retort that if a woman was dry the man wasn't doing his job. He couldn't afford to blow his cover, not now that he knew where Violet was. Protecting her came first.

He choked down the rubbery meatloaf and watery mashed potatoes, then dumped his dishes in the dishwasher and looked for Violet, but she was gone.

Where did she go? His stomach clenched and threatened to send up the sub-par meal he'd just eaten. He waved at the guys and wished them luck, then wandered around the warehouse, trying not to look suspicious.

Nowhere. Violet was nowhere.

Jon knew he needed to calm down, lest he give them away. So, he made his way up the stairs to the roof, where he could watch the water. The door was propped open, and he breathed a sigh of relief when he saw Violet's form silhouetted against the street lamps.

"Hey," he said as he plopped his ass down next to her, shivering against the night wind.

"Dude," she responded, a scowl on her face. "You can't keep following me around like a lost puppy. It looks suspicious."

"But we're best buds now." He gave her a silly grin.

"Norm didn't buy that and no one else will, either. I could see it in his face. First rule of what I do: don't be memorable." She pulled her hood tighter. "I'll see you in the room."

"I was coming up here anyway." He scowled right back. "I couldn't find you."

"See, that's what I'm talking about! You can't do this." She scrubbed a hand over her face, avoiding her beard. "We're about to be in an enclosed space with Jameson and Billy Bob and who knows how many victims. You *cannot* let on something's going on." She groaned. "This is why I shouldn't do this."

"Do what?"

"Get involved with someone when I'm on assignment."

"Are you calling this a mistake?"

"Yes. Yes, I am." Violet stood so fast Jon's head spun. "I'm going back inside. Don't. Follow. Me."

Jon listened to the waves until his bones were freezing. For once, the ocean couldn't bring him peace. She thought they were a mistake. He rubbed at his chest where it hurt, but nothing helped. Once he couldn't stand the cold any longer, he trudged back inside, ready to avoid his roommate.

Chapter 15

VIOLET YAWNED AGAIN AND looked at her watch. She'd been reading for hours, and her body was deciding it was time for bed as dawn broke through the window. They'd be expected to take the ship out at dusk, which she knew from being at NT as long as she had. So she'd better get to bed.

She uncurled herself from the chair in the small lounge area no one frequented. It was time to stop avoiding Jon. His face when she'd told him off had nearly broken her heart, but it had been happening again and she didn't have a good way out of this assignment. She couldn't compromise this job. It wasn't just her ass on the line; it was Jon's and all these captives that she knew were moving through the warehouse.

Just as she reached the stairs, she heard Norm calling. "Victor!"

"Yeah, boss?"

"Homework for you," he told her, and checked to make sure they were alone as he handed her a sheet of paper. "You have to decipher the address you're going to with this code."

"Seriously? You can't just give me the coordinates?"

Norm shook his head. "That's how we do things with this merchandise. It's too valuable to give out coordinates to just anyone. I'm trusting you with this, and only you, understand?" The look on his face told her he expected her to keep the code a secret.

"Understood, sir." Violet swallowed, her mouth suddenly dry. What if she got it wrong?

He must have read the question on her face because he chuckled. "Don't worry, if you can't figure it out, I'll know. We have trackers on the ship to prevent mistakes."

"Great, that makes me feel so much better," she choked out the lie.

"Good lad," he said and slapped her shoulder. She forgot to brace herself in time and he nearly toppled her. She tucked the papers into her hoodie and surreptitiously wiped the sweat from her palms on the inside of the pocket.

"I'll see you later, Norm."

"Don't forget to get the coordinates figured out before you leave. But take notes on your phone and delete them once you get them entered into the navigation system onboard." He got right in her face, an intense glare in his eyes. "Don't leave them around for anyone else to find. Got it?"

"Yes, sir." She gulped, then took the stairs two at a time, her heart thumping in her chest. This puzzle was going to keep her awake until they left, that was for sure.

A quick stop in her dorm room for a change of clothes and then a fast shower later, Violet found herself at the small desk in their room, trying to figure out where they were going.

The door opened and shut, and Jon entered the room. "Vee, we need to talk."

"Later, I'm busy."

"Well, we can't talk in private on the boat."

She sighed and massaged her temples. "I know." If he wanted to talk about their non-relationship again, she might scream.

He sat on the end of her bed and faced the desk. "I can knock Jameson and Billy Bob out, throw them overboard, then we can take off with the boat."

"What about the victims?"

"What about them?"

"We can't just abandon them!" She whispered vehemently. "First off, you're talking about murder, and then the syndicate will just send another boat to the pickup point." She stared back down at the code before her. "Which I have to figure out before we leave."

"Figure out?"

"Norm stopped me on the way up here. He said I have to decode the coordinates and addresses before we can leave." She groaned. "This is like alphabet soup."

"You're smart, Vee, you got this. And I can help, too. ""Don't let Norm know. I'm not supposed to show it to anyone else."

"I won't. Now, back to our escape route—"

"I'm not abandoning them, Jon. That's final."

"Alright." He scrubbed a hand over his face. "We pick up the women, I knock out Jameson and Billy Bob, strap them into life vests," he said pointedly. "I wasn't going to murder them. And then we take the boat and get the women—and us—to safety. You can finish your story, and they can go free."

"Much better. Still don't like that we're dumping two people in the water in winter and they could totally die from hypothermia, but at least it's an improvement over drowning." She rolled her eyes and went back to her task.

"Well, we'll work on it. Maybe we can drop them off on land somewhere."

Violet sighed. "Unfortunately, Norm also mentioned there's a tracker onboard."

Jon shrugged. "Won't be for long. Once we're ready to split, I'll take care of it. I'll shoot a message to Roger and see if Sam can give me some pointers."

"Alright, you work on that, and I'll work on this." Anything to shut him up so she could focus.

Jon disappeared into his phone, his fingers flying. Violet worked through the code for about an hour until she had what she thought were the correct coordinates and address.

"Hey, Jon," she said, startling him. "Can you check this address on your phone? I want to be sure it's real, and I didn't mess this up."

"Sure." He stood and walked over to the desk, his phone in hand. Typing it onto the touch screen, he turned the phone around to show her. "Looks legit."

"Great. I'm going to bed." She tossed back her blanket and slid onto the mattress. It was mid-morning now, and she had to be awake enough to maintain their cover and drive a boat.

"Hey, can I take a picture of this?"

Violet bit her lip. "Do you think it's important?"

Jon nodded. "My brother said their hacker has all of these shipping manifests, but they're written in code. And I really don't want to go anywhere without telling him."

"As long as we don't get caught, I don't care." Her voice slurred from fatigue.

He grinned. "You got it."

The last thing she was aware of was Jon flipping the light and then sleep took her.

Back at Hunt Security Headquarters (a.k.a. Roger's house)...

Roger pinched the bridge of his nose, hoping to nip his headache in the bud. Jenna was due home from the jewelry store any minute, and Sam and Frankie were still upstairs working on the penetration test for his latest cyber security client. Having the two of them on board made those jobs go much faster and smoother, but neither of them were built for dealing with the service side of things.

How had he gone from a soldier to a bodyguard to a customer service agent? Half of these executives didn't understand what they were asking for and the other half thought he understood the jargon they spat out. Thankfully he could take good notes and ask Sam about them. He'd learned more tech speak in the last few months than he'd ever imagined existed. Back in the Army, all that had been Sam's job.

But the money was good, and the customers kept walking away happy. Thank fuck.

Now what was he going to do about lunch? It was his turn to cook.

He picked up his phone and went to scroll through some of the recipes Nadia had sent him when a message from Jon's burner phone came through. The image was a strange handwritten note that made no sense. Roger squinted at the phone, turning it on its side so he could try to figure out what it meant.

Jon: I think this might be helpful. Show it to Frankie. ;)

Holy shit. Holy. Shit. Roger leaped from his desk and ran up the stairs to the office he'd set up for his two computer geniuses. "Frankie! Sam!"

"Tell your boy to stop taking my fucking drinks, Roger, or I quit!"

"Sweetness, I don't want you to spill on your laptop."

Sam and Frankie stood arguing in the middle of the room. Frankie's hands were on her hips and she was glaring up at Sam as he ran a hand through his blonde curls.

This was the opposite of help. "Y'all need to stop arguing and look at this! Jon got the cipher."

They turned to him, and their eyes bugged out at the same time. "Seriously?"

"I'm sending it to both of you. We can finally crack those addresses." The syndicate had been ridiculously careful, hiding the addresses they sent the women to in a complicated code. Frankie and Sam had both tried for ages, but without this equivalent of a decoder ring they'd hit a dead end.

Frankie swayed and then ran to her seat. "I'll start from the top, soldier boy. You start from the bottom."

"I love it when you're on top," Sam responded as he took his station.

"Foreplay later. Decode now." Roger hit send and their phones pinged with the incoming text. "Is there anything I can do to help?"

Sam spoke as his fingers flew. "Call Ross. Get him here."

"And order pizza or something." Frankie cracked her knuckles. "It's going to be a long day and I'm hungry."

"Done."

Just then, the front door opened and closed shut. "Honey, I'm home!"

Roger took the stairs two at a time. "Jenna!"

"Woah there, General." She balked at his enthusiasm. "What's going on?"

He grabbed her shoulders. "Jon got us the cipher."

Her eyes widened. "You're kidding."

"Nope." He waved his phone. "I'm about to call Ross and tell him to get his ass over here. Then I'm ordering pizza."

Jenna held her hand out. "I'll order pizza. Just ask what he wants on it."

Roger slipped his wallet out of his pocket and handed it to her. "Frankie and Sam are working upstairs."

"Got it."

He dialed Ross next. "Hi, Roger."

"Ross, Jon got the cipher."

"Holy shit. Are you sure?"

He called up the stairs. "Yo, Frankie, is it working?"

"It sure is!" she called back.

"You might want to come over. We're ordering pizza. What do you want on it?"

"I'll eat anything but anchovies."

Jenna tapped him on the shoulder and whispered in a hushed voice. "Invite Heather, too!"

He could always count on her to remind him of the appropriate social graces.

"Heather's welcome to join us, too."

Ross chuckled. "Thanks, Roger. I won't be in the doghouse that way."

"Anytime. What does she like on her pizza?"

Ross and Heather arrived five minutes after the pizza did, so everyone was downstairs. Frankie and Sam had the first list of addresses printed off and Frankie had even marked which ones were currently occupied or had hints of upcoming activity.

After scarfing down a few slices, Ross set up his computer in Roger's office and started making phone calls to assemble what might be the biggest simultaneous raid the FBI had ever done.

As the hours wore on into the middle of the night, Frankie handed out her energy drinks. Jenna kept Heather company, watching some crazy home renovation show while Frankie and Sam ran up and down the stairs to hand more addresses to Ross.

Roger was sitting in the living room watching some asshole talk about taking out original built-ins when Ross came in. "So how did your brother get the syndicate's cipher?"

He grimaced. He'd neglected to tell Ross about the job Wanda had sent them on. "Uh, about that..."

"Jon got the job to play Captain Save-A...Reporter." Jenna piped up.

"What?" Ross laughed. "That makes no sense."

Roger let out a breath. Ross wasn't going to like this. "Let's go into the office and I'll explain."

He shut the door behind them and proceeded to relay the story that Wanda had shared when she called him. Ross clenched his eyes shut.

"So let me make sure I have this right. Your brother, a retired Naval officer, is undercover with a fucking reporter and hiding out among the syndicate thugs. Syndicate thugs that I'm about to unleash the *FBI* on?"

Sweat beaded on the back of Roger's neck. "That is correct."

He pressed his fingers against his temples. Roger could have sworn he had steam coming out of his ears. "I need photographs. Now."

Roger happily obliged while Ross sighed and woke his computer up. "We'll have to arrest them with the rest so they can keep their cover, but at the very least I can make sure they're not detained long."

"Thank you." He hit send on the text with the two photos and sheepishly put his phone back in his pocket.

"Don't thank me yet." Ross typed away furiously. "Do you know where they are and where they're going? That would help."

"I know their first stop, not their second. They're probably already there. And based on what we know, there's a chance he can't give me any more information. You saw the camera footage from the houses. I can't think their transports would be any different."

"Shit." Ross wiped a hand over his mouth. "I'll notify everyone. They're supposed to check all their messages before a mission like this, but I can't fix that until after the fact."

"Jon's a big boy. He can handle himself." Roger just hoped that was true for his girl.

Chapter 16

THE TRIP TO THE pickup point was awkward to say the least. Violet didn't know Jameson and Billy Bob, and had no desire to. They left after dinner, Jon in the co-captain's chair while Violet piloted. The others were playing cards down in the galley, *Phase 10* this time.

No one seemed in the mood to socialize with her and Jon.

Jon's knee bounced, and he pushed his hand down to keep it still. Violet looked over at him, then away. She was busy biting the inside of her cheek to calm her nerves.

The silence in the cabin left her a lot of time to think. Jon was sitting right there, temptation in a chair. But she couldn't let him get close again.

Her mother had been at the forefront of her mind lately, wishing she was still here to witness Violet and Callum achieve their dreams. Violet hoped wherever she was that she was at peace and happy. That hopefully, she was proud of them.

Then there was Jon... He'd been her knight in shining armor at the Rusty Nail, always treating her like an actual person instead of a set of tits that served booze like the other patrons in that dive. And knowing now that he'd gone undercover to find her when she'd disappeared made her heart flutter in a funny way in her chest.

She sighed as she recalled her outburst the night before. As much as she ... cared for him, she couldn't do relationships. She couldn't let him get between her and her dreams. Walking away was going to hurt so much worse this time, but she didn't have a choice.

THEY ARRIVED AT THE slip for the pickup just before midnight. Jon exited the boat with Billy Bob and Jameson, both with rifles on their backs, marching up the wooden slats toward a van parked in the lot of a square red building. It looked like a bar on the first floor, with an office above. Another front.

"Do you know who my father is?" came a shrill screech. A guy was holding a thick curvy woman against the van as she fought back, and Jon had to hold himself back from reacting the way he wanted to. He eyed Jameson and Billy. Neither one made a move to help either individual.

Then the thug backhanded her across the face, the crack echoing through the quiet wooded area. "I said shut *up*, bitch!" They continued their approach as the man muttered something at the woman, and she finally cowered away from him.

Jameson crossed his arms and glared at the thug. "Norm said don't damage the merchandise."

He ignored the advice. "This one's mouthy, better watch her."

Billy Bob rubbed his hands together. "Those are the ones that are the most fun to break."

A shudder ran down Jon's spine at his sleazy tone. "It's cold. Let's get moving."

Their point of contact opened the van door and led five more women, and one young man, out of the back. None of them had shoes, nor were they dressed for the weather.

They were bound together by rope, and he attached the last woman to the end of the line.

"Single file. You know the drill. No funny business." Billy and Jameson took the rear guard to keep the captives in line. Jon swallowed as he led them down the dock to the boat where Violet stood on the deck, the ropes to the slip in her hand.

Could he really do this? Could he really allow these criminals to abduct these people and sell their bodies? Jon felt clammy, but he focused on Violet standing there. She became his lighthouse, his north star at the end of that long dock.

He had to do this. They would find a way to get the captives out. But he had to play the game.

The victims didn't give them any more trouble, probably due to the guns, and Billy and Jameson led them down to the bedroom. Seven people crowded in that little room. Jon shook his head as he released the ropes and met Violet back in the bridge where she was programming their next destination.

He pulled out his phone and opened his notes app. They'd already determined that the boat was bugged so they'd decided not to speak anything about their plans out loud, even in a whisper.

Once we're out of sight, he typed on the screen, *I'll find the tracker.* He turned it to show her.

She looked at the phone and nodded. "Course is set," she said out loud.

"Weighing anchor," Jon replied, his hand flipping the switch to pull the anchor back onboard.

He took advantage of the noise and pulled the tool kit he'd pilfered from the maintenance room out of his bag. The boat started up and Violet pulled away. That's when Jon got to work.

Sam had given him a list of places to check for the tracker, saying it would be more effective if it was wired in. They'd discussed how long it took for the boat to be prepared, and he'd advised it was probably hard-wired in behind one of the panels in the helm.

It wasn't difficult to figure out which panel they'd ripped out and put back. Jon ran his fingers over the gouges in the beautiful wood and whimpered. Violet made a sound that sounded like a growl, telling him without words to shut up. He pressed his fingers against the panel and it popped open like no one bothered to be sure it was put back correctly. Once inside, he compared the wires to the diagrams Sam had sent him on his phone.

There. The black box was huge and definitely part of the reason that the panel hadn't shut correctly. It was a simple task to unbolt the tracker from inside the panel and push the panel back into place. But he needed to disable the tracker completely.

That proved to be more difficult. Violet left the helm and grabbed at it, miming throwing it overboard. Jon shook his head. He had a better idea.

He grabbed a hammer from the bag and started going to town on the black plastic casing. It was a lot tougher than it looked. Violet shook her head. "Keep it down!" She whisper-yelled at him.

But Jon was on a mission.

An obnoxious ring went off right above his head and made Jon jump, which smacked his head against the underside of the console. "Ow, fuck!" He rubbed his head as Violet reached for the receiver.

"Hello?"

"What the fuck is going on in there?" Jon could hear Norm yelling without speaker phone, since Violet was holding the receiver away from her head. Jon took it from her. This was his fault, after all.

"What do you mean, sir?"

"The microphones are picking up a lot of banging and the tracker for your ship is going haywire. What are you doing?"

"I found a weird black box on the bridge, sir, didn't know what it was," he lied smoothly, acting like the bumpkin he'd let Norm believe he was.

Norm muttered something about imbeciles and not installing trackers properly. "We need that in case you get lost, White. Now put it back where you found it."

"Yes, sir." Norm hung up the phone and Jon placed theirs back in its holder. "I didn't even see that the last time we were on here."

Violet was seething, her face red with anger. She didn't need words for him to understand he'd fucked up. They'd almost been caught. "You're a motherfucking idiot," she said, putting a finger to her lips. Right, the bugs.

He picked up his phone and typed out another message. *Put her in neutral and come downstairs with your bug sweeper.*

She scowled, but nodded, lowering the anchor and putting the boat in neutral. The engines were still on so it wouldn't raise suspicion with their guard dogs, but they weren't going anywhere.

They walked down the stairs to the galley, where Violet waved her sweeper over every inch of the space. She found three microphones, which Jon relocated to the bridge. When he returned, she was pacing the floor.

"I *told* you we should have thrown it overboard!" She whispered angrily. "Now they're going to be watching us."

"I'm sorry. You were right. But Norm still would have called when we stopped moving on his screen."

"That wouldn't have mattered once we got rid of the other two. Now we'll be watched even more closely."

"Do you think he'd call Jameson or Billy to take over?"

She shook her head. "They don't have the coordinates."

He sank onto the banquette, rubbing a hand over his face. "We need a new plan."

Violet crossed her arms over her chest and glared at him. "We didn't have a plan in the first place. This was all your big idea."

She was right. He'd acted alone with tampering with the tracker and it had cost them time and trust. Both things they couldn't afford to lose. "We could throw all three of them overboard along with the satellite phone so he couldn't call."

"They'd die!" She threw her hands up in the air. "I can't have that on my hands."

Jon shrugged. "Syndicate scum, they deserve it. But okay." He raised his hands in the universal position of surrender. "You take the lead on this." As much as it pained him, he wanted a future with her after this and he wouldn't let his ego get in the way of that.

Frankie hunched over her makeshift desk, her fingers flying over the keyboard. Three empty energy drink cans stood sentinel around her workspace, a testament to the incredible night and day they'd had. But her eyes were getting bleary in the early light. Ross had taken his fiancée home hours ago.

She'd had the best idea, though. While she'd compiled lists of addresses for the raid, she'd realized Jon's cipher had been useful in more than one way. The syndicate had kept meticulous records of who had utilized their services, or just purchased a slave outright. It was probably for future blackmail purposes.

Their records of their victims were far less detailed. It'd be impossible to find them all if they weren't still held captive. But she swallowed the bile down instead of thinking too hard on that.

How many times had these predators gotten away with their crimes due to influence and money? While Ross believed the syndicate's inner circle would pay dearly, the same couldn't be said for their customers. And the customers, in Frankie's mind, were just as guilty. After all, if there were no market for such a heinous trade there would be no sex trafficking.

No more. Frankie had been failed by the system too many times to leave this to the authorities. She'd share what she found with Ross, of course. But that wasn't all she was going to do.

Snickering to herself, Frankie was so in her zone that a tap on her shoulder made her jump nearly out of her chair.

"What the—oh it's just you." Her boyfriend, Sam, leaned over her and stared at her screen with blue eyes that carried as much baggage as hers did.

"You didn't hear me knock."

"Clearly." She turned back to her screen, but his pale hands came down over her dark brown ones. The rainbow lights of her keyboard lit them up like a rave.

"Come to bed, little hacker. You can finish whatever this is in the afternoon." Roger and Jenna had long since gone to bed themselves, telling Frankie and Sam to crash in the second guest room.

"Afternoon?" She looked up at him, confused.

"It's eight in the morning."

"Oh. Time flies when you're saving the world."

He furrowed his brows. "What are you doing? We got Ross all the addresses."

"But that's not all the *evidence*." Frankie rolled her head back as his hands began to massage her shoulders and all the adrenaline fell away. All of a sudden, she could feel every last one of the past thirty-six hours catching up to her.

"What else did you find?"

"Names. Transactions." She smiled like the cat that got the cream and closed her eyes. "I got the receipts."

"So the FBI can arrest more than just the syndicate?" Sam turned her chair around and knelt to put himself at her eye level.

Frankie gave him a sly smirk. "Maybe."

"Francesca...." His voice was a warning. "What are you going to do?"

She shrugged her shoulders and his eyebrow rose. "Wouldn't it be a shame if the media got a hold of the list of people who paid for those women and men? If those shady transactions suddenly saw the light?"

He shook his blond curls even as his eyes sparked at her mischief. "Share it with Ross, too, will you?"

Her voice hardened. "No shit. But I don't see why people should get to make plea deals and stay out of the spotlight. They ruined people's lives, too. Why shouldn't they face justice?"

One side of his mouth lifted as he fought a smile, his hands coming down over her fists that she hadn't realized she'd clenched. "I bet Wanda would have some contacts."

She wrapped her arms around his neck and leaned in with a purr. "I love the way you think, soldier boy."

Sam chuckled and pressed his lips to her temple. "The world will be there after we sleep, sweetness."

"I know," she whined, "but I want to get this done."

"After you rest. You want to make sure all those names are accurate."

Her shoulders dropped. Damn it, he was right. If she was going to ruin lives, she wanted to make sure they were actually guilty. "Ugh, fine. Let me save the file." She spun in her chair and saved her file, then put her laptop to sleep.

Sam herded her toward the guest room she'd once stayed in on an air mattress. Roger had upgraded since she'd moved in with Sam, getting a proper mattress when his little brother came to stay with him after coming home from war. She changed for bed, then groaned as she lay down. Her body was protesting her working so long.

"Do we need to get you one of those standing desks?" Sam chuckled as he slid in next to her in just his boxers.

"I should probably see a chiropractor once this this over."

Sam snorted. "You hate doctors."

"A chiropractor is not a doctor. They're completely different jobs."

"Whatever you say, sweetness." He nuzzled into her neck, avoiding her satin bonnet. "Get some sleep."

His steady breathing made the voice in the back of her head saying "*Release the files*" go quiet.

She'd release the files, alright. Later.

Chapter 17

VIOLET COLLAPSED ONTO THE bench next to him. "You'd really kill them?"

Jon shrugged. "If the choice is kill or be killed, I know which side I don't want to be on." He wrapped an arm around her shoulders. "And I respect your integrity. So no, I won't throw them over."

She scrubbed her hands over her eyes, finding it hard to draw breath even though her body felt hollow. "I've never done a story where so much was on the line. It's never been this dangerous before."

Jon raised an eyebrow. "You exposed a drug ring linked to the cartels in Mexico."

"It's not like the *cartel* was in Maryland," she said with a roll of her eyes. "I didn't have to get this deep for that story."

"You got this, Vee." He craned his head over to look at the hatch that led to the stairs. "The door shut?"

"Yeah, why?"

"Because I want to do this." He grasped her chin between his fingers and turned her head, sealing his mouth over hers.

He swallowed her surprised cry. Jon didn't wrap his arms around her, just held her in his thrall with nothing but his lips and that clever tongue until she had to come up for air.

"What was that for?" She blinked at him.

"You were right. I'm sorry. You tried to stop me and I didn't listen."

Her chest tightened. "Your heart was in the right place. But we're risking more than just our lives here, you get that?"

"Yeah, Nellie, I do." A warm smile spread across his face and her heart melted as he called her by her idol's name. "You're beautiful. Brave. Bad ass." He punctuated each compliment with another kiss.

The walls she'd spent the last twelve hours building back up came crashing down. Fuck, she never would have guessed faith in her would be such an aphrodisiac.

"Jon, we can't..."

"That hatch is soundproof, baby. They don't want anyone hearing whatever might be going on down there. I overheard one of the guys talking about it." He leaned over her, and Violet should have felt intimidated, but her traitorous body wanted him closer. With fewer clothes on.

"The mics are upstairs. No one will know." He stroked her cheek with his palm. "I have to say, I've never kissed anyone with a beard before."

She tried to swallow her laugh. "We can't let them see a used condom in the trash."

"I'll flush it down the toilet."

"You'll have to get past them with it." Violet rubbed her thighs together, praying for some relief. But it wasn't enough. She needed more. She needed him. "I got the shot right before I came on this assignment. So, if you're clean, I'm good."

His pupils nearly swallowed the green in his eyes as they dilated at the idea. "I am. Are you sure?"

"Yes. But we have to be quick. And quiet."

No sooner had the words left her mouth than he nudged her off the bench. "Lift your shirt and lie down." She did as he suggested, pulling her t-shirt and hoodie up to expose her breasts. He lifted his shirt as well, pulling it off, then stuffing the hem in her mouth.

"Just in case. Okay?" She agreed with a nod, then his mouth and hands were on her, ravishing her as she struggled to stay quiet. The cotton grew damp in her mouth, muffling her gasps and moans as he pinched her nipples and sent bolts of lightning straight to her clit.

She squirmed and punched her hips upward to make her point. *Fuck me already,* they said. They didn't have time to draw this out.

Jon's hands slid down her sides to her waist, unbuttoning her jeans and pulling the zipper down. He shoved the denim down past her knees, then propped her legs open and released himself from his own pants. She managed to get one leg free so she could wrap her legs around his hips, but he suddenly stopped and stared.

What was he doing?

He leaned over and propped himself over her, close so she could hear. "I've never gone bare before."

Oh. Oh, goodness. Neither had she, but Violet hadn't thought of that when she'd suggested it. She spat the shirt out. "We don't have to if you don't want to."

Jon shook his head. "I do want to. More than anything. I just wish we were doing this on a bed somewhere."

She grinned. "You don't think the risk of getting caught makes it that much hotter?"

He thought for a moment. "It's a bit dangerous in this scenario but I'm not saying no."

Violet chuckled. "Danger is my middle name."

Jon grinned down at her. "I love it."

Then he slid his heated length slowly into her. His mouth dropped open and his eyes rolled back in his head as he savored every inch.

Violet's heart tried to pound out of her chest. Skin on skin felt so different, smoother, warmer, than with a latex barrier between them. Jon thrust in and out agonizingly slow, never moving his face more than a few inches from hers. Violet stared into his eyes as he drove in and out, a look of wonder on his face that mirrored her soul.

They got lost in each other's gaze, never looking away. Violet wasn't even sure she blinked as he made love to her while the ocean rocked the boat.

In spite of, or maybe because of the dangerous situation they found themselves in, her heart raced and time stood still. Nothing else existed but them and this moment. But she could never have this again. She let herself swim in the sensations, not wanting to miss a single moment. Because if they made it out of the syndicate alive, she'd have to walk away.

She closed her eyes, turning her head so he wouldn't see her fighting not to cry. Her peak built and built and built until it crashed over her like a wave on the shore, drenching everything in its wake. Jon wasn't far behind her, his heat filling her as he gave a soft groan.

He stroked a hand over her head as he lay above her, not moving until his cock had softened to the point it fell out of her. Before he pushed himself off, he laid a gentle kiss on her mouth, then rose on shaky legs to gather napkins from the galley. The paper was rough on her sensitized skin, but she appreciated how it brought her back to reality.

She was on a boat bound for the syndicate with rifle-toting watchdogs.

They righted their clothes and Jon disposed of the evidence, opening a window to let the sea air wash away the scent of sex.

Violet stretched, her well-worked body humming with pleasure. "We better get going before Norm calls again."

"Yeah. But I need cuddles first." He gathered her into his arms and held on tight.

"Jon! We can't get caught."

He stared down at her and smoothed his hand through her hair. "I won't let anything happen to you, Vee. Because when I look at you, I see forever."

Her heart stuttered. Forever? Surely, he didn't mean that. No one would want forever with her crazy job. Any man would want to change her, make her smaller, give up her dreams. They didn't want a woman who put herself in danger all the time. It wasn't like she'd hadn't tried relationships before, back in college. But that was always how they ended. And she couldn't — she *wouldn't*—let a relationship take her down the path of ruin like she'd seen happen to so many of her colleagues.

Provided she survived this crazy mess she'd gotten herself into. She still had to figure out how to rescue the captives with Norm and the syndicate tracking their every move.

She'd have to walk away all over again. An ache in her chest bloomed at the realization. And it would hurt him so much worse this time, now that he knew who she was. Violet couldn't do forever with him. Would he let her go?

The stress would eat her alive if she kept thinking about it. So, she did what she did best: bury herself in her work.

"Come on, Navy boy. Let's get back before Norm skins us."

Jon followed her up the stairs back to the bridge in a daze. His Vee was amazing. A bit crazy but amazing. He wondered if she could bring him as a bodyguard for all of her assignments, though he hoped she wouldn't take on one quite as dangerous as this for a while. He'd need a break.

If it wasn't possible, maybe she'd let him show her some self-defense moves. He, Roger, and Finn had all taught Nadia how to defend herself for the times they weren't around. They could teach Violet. Maybe even get her a concealed carry permit. He'd never want to squash her spirit, but he'd worry a lot less if he knew she could defend herself when push came to shove.

It was a good thing he wasn't behind the controls, because he still couldn't think straight after burying himself in her heat with nothing between them. He'd never felt anything like it, like her. A connection had formed between them in that moment that he slid inside, that he could never have gotten with anyone else. Because it was Violet, the one that got away, that was handing over that piece of herself. She had to feel it, too—after too many years of uniform chasers, he wouldn't have trusted anyone else to tell the truth about her birth control. Though he'd taken care of it himself years ago, it meant a lot that she'd thought ahead. He'd rather suffer blue balls than risk getting tied to anyone he didn't love.

He'd almost slipped and told her, too. But she was skittish about their relationship. She'd already called it a mistake once. Jon knew though, that her mind just needed time to catch up. It was clear her body was on board. And he was pretty sure that her heart was, too.

Steps coming up the stairs alerted him they weren't alone anymore. "Yo, Vic, what's our ETA?"

"Had to stop and deal with something," Violet answered Jameson. "Should only be a couple more hours."

"Everything alright?"

"Yeah, everything's fine. I'll come get you when we're docked."

They didn't talk much at all on the trip back to Nautical Transit, mindful of the microphones. Let Norm think Victor was pissed off at him. It would only drive home the point that Jon had been acting alone, and therefore protect Violet.

Chapter 18

It was the middle of the night when Violet, her eyes bleary, piloted the boat into the warehouse dock. She killed the engine and slumped in her chair as Jon went out on the deck to tie them down.

Her nerves felt raw and her chest ached with the knowledge she'd been forced to bring those captives back with her. Damn Norm for sending them with watchdogs. If it had been just her and Jon, she'd have thrown the tracker overboard with the satellite phone. But having the other two aboard meant they had to tow the line. And now she had to go downstairs and act like it didn't bother her that it was time to unload the captives.

She marched down the stairs, past the galley, to the lowest deck, where Billy Bob and Jameson were playing *Phase 10* outside the bedroom again. The lock on the door was new. No noise came from inside the room, and Violet wondered if that had been soundproofed as well, or if the captives just knew making noise was pointless.

Swallowing her guilt and her nausea, she spoke. "We're here."

Billy rose with a groan. "Good, this guy is kicking my ass."

Jameson cleaned up his cards with a grin. "Better luck next time."

"What now?" Violet shoved her hands into her hoodie pocket.

"Let's go ask Norm where he wants 'em." Billy Bob shouldered his rifle and headed up the stairs. "You stay with the boat, Vic."

"Okay." Violet followed them upstairs at a leisurely pace and stood next to Jon on the deck to watch them go off in search of the boss.

"What happens now?" he asked her.

"They're gonna check with Norm and find out."

The hairs on the back of her neck stood straight up. "Jon..." her voice reverted to its normal tone. "Something's not right."

He scowled into the warehouse. "Where is everyone?"

That's when she heard it. "FBI! Come out with your hands up!"

Gun shots echoed within the building, and the warehouse erupted into chaos. Norm came flying down the stairs and headed straight for them. "Get that boat out of here!" he yelled.

Violet looked at Jon, then back at Norm. "Where am I taking it?"

Sweat dripped down the older man's face, his cheeks ruddy as he gasped for breath. "I don't care where you take it! They can't find the..." His eyes flitted to the boat, and she realized he wanted them to hide the captives from the authorities.

Fucking scumbucket.

Jon grabbed her arm. "Come on, Vic." He pulled her down with him to untie the boat, not that you needed two people. "I left the mics on the co-captain's chair. Sweep for the rest while I get us untied." He spoke low so no one else would overhear. It might not be necessary since Norm had already run off.

"Where are we taking them?"

He stared right into her eyes. "Where do you think?" Then he winked. "Let's move."

Violet hurried inside to do as he said, sweeping for the mics that she knew had been planted. She found one by the stairwell and one by the wheel. Gathering them all in her hands, she plunged them deep into a small pocket in her bag, in case they needed them for evidence.

Then she started up the boat as Jon slid into the chair next to hers. "Did you get them all?"

"Yeah. Hid them so they can't hear anything else."

"Smart. Might need them for evidence."

"That's what I was thinking."

She gunned the motor, not caring that she left a hell of a wake behind them. She sure as hell wasn't going to clean it up.

Jon was on his cell phone, and he put it on speaker so she could hear. "Roger! Did you send the FBI in there?"

A chuckle came over the line. "Ross has your names and pictures. You won't be in actual trouble."

"Well, I got a present for Ross," Jon told him.

"Oh?"

"We got a boatload of captives. Tell us where to land this thing."

"I'll drop you a pin for my location. We're not far from the water."

"We're gonna need a dock of some kind." Violet reminded Jon.

"Who's with you?"

"Violet Giordano, dressed as a guy."

"Thank fuck," Roger said, relief evident in his voice. "Wanda wasn't satisfied with your earlier report and she's been hounding me daily."

"Tell her she better send me in for a Pulitzer for this story!" Violet called.

"You got it. Jon, did you get my location?"

"Roger that. Let me put the coordinates in and we'll get as close as we can."

"I'll tell Ross and we'll head toward the water."

"See you soon, Big Bro." Jon's grin was infectious.

"This sounds like it's going to get tricky," Violet said. "Why don't you take over and I'll go inform the captives what's going on?"

"Sounds good, Nellie." He licked his lips and leaned forward. "When this is over, I'm going to kiss the hell out of you."

All Violet could do was laugh. "Let me go warn them. They've had enough shock and we need them to stick with us while we take them to safety."

He gave her a salute. "Aye, aye, Captain."

She lifted the hatch and jogged down to the lowest deck. At the very least, she could let them wander around a bit and stretch their legs.

Violet slid the lock on the door open and knocked. She could hear murmurs from behind the door.

"Since when do these guys knock?"

"They locked us in here, and now they're knocking?"

"The lock's open," she called out. "I'm not really with the syndicate."

The door cracked open to reveal a thick, deep-skinned woman with wary eyes. "What's going on? We heard shots."

"The FBI raided the warehouse."

"And you drove us away, why?"

"Norm, the guy in charge, told us to. He didn't want them to find you. So, we decided to launch a rescue." She picked at the edge of her beard, showing the other woman that it wasn't real. "My name's not actually Victor. It's Violet Giordano."

At the realization Violet wasn't with the syndicate, the door opened wider. Seven pairs of eyes stared back at her from inside.

The elected spokeswoman crossed her arms. "What are you doing here?"

"I'm a journalist with InVestigate. We got a tip that Nautical Transit was up to no good, so I was undercover." She pointed up the stairs. "Driving the boat is my ... friend Jon, who was also undercover. We're taking you to the FBI so you can go home." Friend. That's what they were going to have to be satisfied with when all this was through. But she needed to focus on the victims now.

"For real? You're not playin' with us?" She glared at Violet.

"I swear to you. We're getting you out of here." Violet hesitated. "What's your name?"

"Myesha."

"Myesha, you're not captive anymore. Come on upstairs while Jon takes us to the meeting point." She waved them up, pointing at the galley. "I think there are still some water bottles in the fridge, and there's more space."

One by one, the captives cautiously left the bedroom. None of them had clothes appropriate for the weather. God, she hoped they didn't get frostbite in the chilly February night.

She ran back up to the bridge. "Jon, call your brother. These guys can't go wading through the water. It's too cold."

"It's okay, Vee." He turned to her. "Roger found a boat launch close by, and the FBI is sending transportation."

"Great. I hope they have socks with them."

"We'll survive." Myesha had joined them on the bridge. Apparently, everyone wanted to explore the trawler, and

Violet couldn't blame them. The boat had been a luxurious ride once, long before the syndicate bought it.

The boat launch came into view ahead, and Jon steered the boat as close as he could. A man that looked remarkably like Jon but with a short beard, waved from where he stood next to a silver pickup truck. Next to that was a black van, a shorter man in a bulletproof vest with FBI painted across it exiting the driver's side.

"There's Roger." Jon pulled them up alongside the launch and dropped the anchor. "Let's go see how we need to do this."

She followed him out onto the deck, wrapping her arms around herself. "Damn, it's cold."

"Yeah, I left the van running so the heat's on." The man that didn't look like Jon called up. "Which one of you is Jon and which one is Violet?"

Roger pointed up at Jon. "That one's my brother."

She raised her hand. "I'm Violet." After a beat, she added. "The beard is fake."

"That explains a lot," she thought she heard Roger say. "Jon, this is Agent Ross Patterson, our contact at the Bureau."

"Nice to meet you!" Jon called out and waved.

"How many on board?" Patterson asked.

"Seven besides us," Violet answered. "And none of them are dressed for this weather."

"We expected as much based on what Josie told us. I've got some blankets in the van. But I gotta get back to the warehouse so we can finish up this raid. A couple assholes haven't come out yet, so we're having to hunt through the maze."

"Shit." She turned to Jon. "Do you think Norm will run?"

"Wouldn't put it past him," he said, straightening up. "How do y'all want us to get them down there?"

Roger lifted a ladder out of his truck and hefted it onto his shoulder. "I was hoping this would be a smaller boat."

Jon shrugged. "It's as good a plan as any."

"I can see if there's any rope. We could slide down." Violet gnawed on her lip. Would the ladder be tall enough?

"Let's try this. It might be more stable," Jon said to her, then hollered down to his brother. "Why do you have Dad's ladder in your truck?"

"It's not Dad's ladder, it's my ladder. I literally just picked it up from the hardware store when Ross called and said they were launching the raid and asked if I wanted to be there to keep your sorry ass out of jail." Violet snickered at the brotherly banter. She needed to call Callum as soon as she got back to her phone. Roger lifted the ladder and opened it. "It's a twenty-four footer."

"Why do you need such a tall ladder?"

"*Some*one has to clean the gutters on my house." Roger rolled his eyes. "Ross, come over here and stand behind it. I don't want anyone to fall."

The ladder actually came up to the railing, which was a relief. Ross and Roger stabilized it and then Violet waved the captives out from the galley. "Who wants to go first?"

Myesha stepped up, her bare feet curling against the frigid deck. Violet helped guide her onto the ladder, where she slowly descended, Roger and Ross hanging onto it for dear life. When she jumped down, the shakes overtook her. "Can you make it to that van up there, sweetheart? The door's open and the heat's on." Ross's voice was gentle. Myesha nodded and hurried away.

"Jon, why don't you get down there and then you can help? I'll stay up here."

He nodded. "Sounds good, Vee." He called down to his brother. "I'm gonna come next, I can give piggyback rides up to the van." To Violet, he said, "Who knows what kinda shit is laying on this launch?" She nodded, and watched as he scurried down the ladder, running up to Myesha to offer his services. Thankfully, she took him up on it, and he ran up the boat launch with her on his back.

Fuck, he was adorable. The walls around her heart were crumbling, fast.

Steeling herself, Violet turned to the rest of the group. "Who's next?"

JON DELIVERED THE FREED captives to the FBI van one by one, getting them into the warmth as quickly as possible. Ross had brought a couple of packs of warm socks, which they distributed among themselves. Good; no one would lose a toe tonight. He turned the keys to the boat over to Ross, who said that the FBI would confiscate it as evidence.

They agreed to meet back on the FBI side of the raid against the warehouse. Jon and Violet would need to give statements, and until that happened, they couldn't go home. Ross had a full van, so the two of them rode back in Roger's truck.

"You never did explain to me how the hell you got involved with FBI." Jon looked at his brother. "And why didn't you call him when we got the call from Wanda?"

"Sam knows him and brought him in after we rescued Josie. He took point on her case. The FBI's had their eye on the syndicate for a while now, just getting all the pieces together took time." He glanced at Jon, then back at the road. "That cipher broke everything wide open."

"It did?" Violet asked from the backseat. He'd tried to insist she take the front, but she said he should sit with his brother.

"Yep."

Jon shook his head. "Norm gave it to Violet. I wasn't even supposed to see it."

"Frankie had hacked into their servers and found the shipping manifests, but they were written in code and she couldn't find the method to decode it. Once I gave it to her, she and Sam were up all night translating the addresses. I called Ross and he organized a giant raid across the country. Every safe house and warehouse got hit at the same time."

"Damn. That's some operation." Jon's head spun.

"He thinks it's the biggest one they've ever done. But he and his superiors were determined that the trafficking and kidnappings ended tonight."

"Were they successful?" Violet leaned forward so her head was between them.

"As far as I know no one's failed. But we're at a stalemate. There are still a few people unaccounted for."

Violet sounded thoughtful. "Norm was still in there when we left."

Roger pulled his truck up next to Ross's black van, the man in question already outside and speaking to another agent, a woman. When they walked up to him, he was patting her on the shoulder.

"Thanks, Horne. See you at the safe house."

"See you, boss." Then she got into the van with the freed captives and drove away.

"Where are they going?" Violet looked at the van's disappearing taillights.

"I don't want them anywhere near this tonight. They've been traumatized enough." Ross cracked his knuckles. "Graham got us a map of this place, but it's a goddamn maze. It's taking forever to flush these guys out."

"Who's missing?"

"A lot of them, including the boss, Norm."

"Of course. Fucking coward." Jon's upper lip lifted in disgust. He'd like to spit in Norm's eye for what he'd perpetuated.

"He's probably going to make a break for it," Violet said thoughtfully. "But he'd want to get his hard drive first." Her voice trailed off, deep in thought.

"I need that evidence. Show me where his office is," Ross waved them over.

Jon looked over the blueprint. "It's on the first floor," he said. Ross shuffled the papers around until they were looking at the right one.

He traced the path with his finger that he'd taken to get to Norm's office. "It should be around here."

Ross lifted the walkie-talkie to his mouth. "Agent Barnhart, have you searched quadrant 1-C yet?"

"Negative," the response crackled with static. "Still encountering resistance."

"Intel says the boss should be there."

"Copy that."

Jon stood there with Ross, surveying the warehouse surrounded by agents and portable floodlights. Vans with handcuffed suspects, agents in riot gear.

This was more action than he'd been hoping for. Good thing it wasn't his job.

He shivered in the night air and remembered Violet was only wearing a hoodie. "Vee, you alright?" Jon turned to take her in his arms and keep her warm. But Violet wasn't there.

"Where did she go?"

Fuck, had she run from him *again*?

Chapter 19

VIOLET CREEPED ALONG THE edges of the chaos, blending into the night. She had to get to the side door of the warehouse. Norm would escape with that hard drive and then the FBI wouldn't be able to pin anything on the syndicate. She hadn't worked for him a long time but she knew his type. He'd do anything to keep himself out of hot water, even throw the rest of them under the bus. And this syndicate, like all organized crime, was like a cancer — if you didn't snuff the whole thing out, it would grow back.

Apparently, no one guarded the door that faced the woods. The agents probably figured no one would come in after them and the thugs were all either hiding or in custody. The building would be in an uproar as the agents swept every floor. But she only had to get in to the first floor.

Eerie silence met her ears as she scurried through the yellow painted hall. Gunshots echoed from one of the floors above her. Good. That told her they were nowhere near here. She flew down the hallway, her sneakers barely making contact with the floor. The light in Norm's office was dark, the frosted glass obscuring her view. She checked the handle; locked of course. But Violet was no amateur. She pulled a paperclip from her pocket that she'd always kept on her since as Victor she couldn't carry her purse with her lock picking tools. After pulling it apart, she kneeled on the floor and pressed it into the lock.

She had to jiggle it around a bit to find the right spot, and then with just enough pressure... click! The handle swung down when she pulled on it this time, and she slipped into the room, shutting and locking the door behind her.

Norm's computer never slept, its indicator lights twinkling in the darkness. She couldn't sneak that desktop out of there, but she knew he never kept anything on it; after doing data entry her first week there she'd learned that everything was on the black box next to it. Hopefully, it was up to date and it wouldn't matter that she didn't have time to eject it properly. It was a simple matter of locating the cords and pulling them. The computer let out a low whine that indicated something had been unplugged. Violet stashed the drive in her hoodie pocket and then followed the wires to the floor where the power strip was. The FBI would need the cord to access the files.

Then footsteps echoed in the corridor, voices following close behind. Shit! She scrambled to hide under the desk, abandoning her quest for the wires.

Please let them pass. Please let them pass. Please let them pass...

A key clicked into a lock, and then came the creak of a door opening. When the lights came on above her head, Violet knew she was in deep shit.

"Turn that out, you moron! I don't want the Feds finding us before we can get out of here."

"Sorry, boss."

Violet didn't dare blink. She breathed as shallowly as possible, since holding her breath was a dumb idea.

"I'll grab this drive, then we'll get to the van. What the..." Violet bit her lip as Norm swore a blue streak. "Where is the motherfucking hard drive? How did it disappear?"

"It's not here?"

"No, it's supposed to be right on my desk! No one else has access to this office, so *where the fuck did it go?*" he bellowed.

Violet's heart pounded in her chest. Somehow, they still hadn't seen her. But all Norm had to do was sit in his desk chair and the jig would be up.

JON AND ROGER SEARCHED through the chaos, looking everywhere for Violet. He'd gone left and Roger had gone right, and they met back at Ross's center command, both empty-handed.

"Where could she have gone?" Jon wiped his clammy hands on his jeans and tried to keep his cool. Losing his shit wouldn't get Violet back. He turned to Ross. "Did someone arrest her by mistake?"

Ross shook his head. "I comm'ed all the agents. No one's seen her."

"Shit." Jon scrubbed a hand through his hair.

Roger looked at him with concern. "Jon, do you think... she'd go back?"

"What? No!" But then the blood drained from his face as he considered how important this story was to Violet. "Wait… She said something about Norm not leaving without his hard drive." He gripped his hair as realization dawned on him. "Fuck! She's gotta be after the drive!" It would be the evidence both she and the FBI needed to pin these crimes on Norm and the syndicate. He turned, but before he could make a run for the door, Ross had grabbed him by the collar.

"Hunt, there's no way I'm letting you in there. You're a civilian now and neither one of you should have gone back. Let the pros handle it."

Jon spun around, a small ripping sound accompanying the move. "That's. My. Girl." He nearly shouted at the FBI agent, pointing back at the warehouse. Ross smacked a palm across his face and sighed.

"These brothers of yours, Roger, I swear…"

"I'm with him," Roger said in a firm voice. "He can get in without arousing suspicion."

"So can I," came a familiar voice from behind Jon. He spun around again.

"Jameson?!" What was that asshole doing here?

The man known as Jameson lifted a badge up to Jon's eye level. "It's actually Agent Luke Graham. You and Ms. Giordano weren't the only ones undercover."

Ross sounded like he'd lost control of the whole situation. "Graham…"

"It's fine, boss. I can go in with him. The other agents won't shoot us once they see me."

That ... was a complication Jon hadn't considered. *I'm an idiot,* he thought to himself.

Ross waved them forward with a huge sigh. "Fine. But no heroics."

"Sure thing, boss." Jameson gave him a jaunty salute. "You coming?"

"One sec." Roger stepped forward and gave Jon a one-armed hug while a heavy weight dropped into his hoodie pocket. "I prefer to ask for forgiveness rather than permission." When he drew back, he winked, and Jon slid his hand inside his pocket to discover Roger's Glock. He grinned.

"Thanks, Brother." Turning to the agent formerly known as Jameson, he nodded. "Let's go."

Jon no longer felt the cold as he jogged along behind Graham, his companion nodding when his fellow agents acknowledged him. Violet better be in there. And when he got her alone, he was going to spank her ass again for scaring him. When they approached the front door, Graham spoke quietly into his comm.

"Barnheart, I'm coming back in with one of the informants. We're looking for a drive."

"Roger that."

He pulled open the door which was flanked by two agents in riot gear. "After you."

The dingy yellow walls echoed with their footsteps and the distant sound of gunshots above them on another floor. Since they'd both been undercover here, Jon and Graham didn't need to discuss where they were going, making their way on silent feet toward the office.

Halfway there, Jon picked up the shouting. "Uh oh," he muttered.

"Fuck stealth," came Graham's reply.

Jon had to agree. They broke out into a run, the agent keeping pace with him the whole way down the hall. He could hear Norm's yelling but couldn't make out the exact words until they were almost on top of the office.

"You little shit! You think you can steal from me? From this organization? Do you have a death wish?"

Violet!

Jon had his hand around the Glock when Graham grabbed his arm. "Let me do the talking."

Sweat beaded on Jon's forehead, his hands trembling with rage. But no, Graham was right. In this op, Graham was above him in the chain of command. He had to let the professional take over so they could get Violet out.

Nodding, Jon followed Graham through the open door. The lights weren't on but enough light came in from the hallway for him to see two thugs holding Violet by the arms, red marks on her face and her left eye starting to swell.

Graham placed a hand on his chest as he started to growl. Shit, he couldn't do that. He had to keep his head.

"You're still here, Norm? I thought you'd be long gone by now."

"I had to get my hard drive. But I caught Victor here stealing it!" He turned back to Violet. "I told you and John to drive the boat away!"

He spoke before he thought better of it. "We did! It's safe."

Norm looked back at Jon and did a double take. "Now, what the fuck are you *both* doing back here?"

"The boat is safe, Norm, and so is the merchandise." Graham picked up his ploy with practiced ease. "Vic and John came back to make sure everyone got out okay, and to make sure your hard drive was safe."

"There's no getting out now," one of the thugs said nervously. Jon couldn't remember what that one's name was. "Not unless we swim for it."

"I'm not swimming with a valuable hard drive!" Norm palmed his face. "I have another boat."

"Really, boss?"

"Yeah. A boat for one, dipshit."

"But boss!" they cried as one, both of them dropping Violet in their distress.

"Don't 'boss' me. It's every man for himself in the syndicate." Norm gripped the hard drive and turned to the door. "The two of you can stay here and take the fall since you can't be bothered to actually do as you're told. Now I have to hunt down a boat full of merchandise before the Feds find it."

Graham looked at Jon and then angled his head ever so slightly toward the two goons. Jon dropped his head in a barely perceptible nod.

The minute Norm slipped the drive into his pocket, Graham tackled him. Jon raised his gun and aimed between Tweedle Dee and Tweedle Dumb as Violet ran to his side. But the goons didn't make any move to help their boss.

Graham slapped his cuffs on Norm and pulled him to his feet. Then he flashed his badge at him and the thugs. "I'm not Jameson. I'm FBI. Are you two going to come quietly or do I need to get the zip ties?"

Both of them raised their hands in surrender with resigned looks on their faces. Graham nodded. He led Norm out the door first. "Jon, you take the rear."

Right. Cause he had his gun out. The trouble twins, not that they looked remotely alike, but that's what he was calling them, followed Norm, and Jon was close behind with Violet walking next to him.

"Jon... thank you..."He shook his head. "Later. Away from these guys." She nodded.

The warehouse was quiet as they exited out into the night. The floodlights nearly blinded him, but he didn't leave Graham until they had the twins in cuffs as well, and he gestured for him to go back to Roger and Ross. Jon put his gun away and then he took Violet by the chin and looked over her face.

"Baby, what were you thinking going in alone?"

She teared up, and stabbing pains burst in his chest. "I just didn't want him getting away. I knew the drive was important, and I was worried..."

Jon pulled her into his arms, and she yelped, pushing him away. He released her immediately. All thoughts of punishing her fled.

"What did that asshole do to you?" he growled. His muscles tensed, his eyes seeking out where the agent had dragged Norm off to. Surely no one would care if he got in a few shots of his own...

"Kicked me in the ribs when he found me hiding under the desk." She grimaced. "I don't think anything's broken. I'm just sore." Violet was squinting through one eye more than the other, and he knew that swollen eye was going to be a spectacular bruise.

"You're going to have quite the shiner tomorrow."

She sighed. "I know."

"Just please, don't disappear like that on me again. What if we hadn't realized where you'd gone?"

"I'm sorry." Her eyes watered, and she started to shiver. Either her adrenaline was about to crash, or she was going into shock.

He wrapped her back up, careful of his arms this time. "I would have gone back in with you." Then he snorted. "Although Ross is not going to be happy with either of us."

She chuckled, then groaned. "I guess we better face the music." She started to pull away, and he stopped her with a hand to her shoulder. Her cheek was too bruised for him to risk touching it.

"Hey, we got him. We got all of them. And that's what counts."

"And the captives are free." Her lower lip began to tremble. He could feel his own adrenaline crash coming as well, and he needed to get his girl somewhere safe.

"Let's go back to Ross, give our statements, and then I'll get Roger to take us to a hotel." She let out a shaky breath and nodded.

A realization washed over him. One of calm and caring and... love. He'd thought he'd loved her four years ago. But that had been a mere infatuation with a character she played. This was the real Violet: a crazy danger-seeking missile that wanted to expose the world's crimes. And he loved her.

But he wasn't going to tell her in the middle of an FBI raid.

Chapter 20

HOURS LATER, VIOLET FOLLOWED Jon into the hotel room and nearly fell face-first onto the bed.

"Thank God that's over." She dropped her bag on the floor and dug for her wig glue remover. Her face was never going to be the same. And she was never pretending to be a guy again.

"You can say that again." Jon threw his own bag next to hers. The only option had been two queen beds, and they hadn't discussed sleeping arrangements yet.

"Take whichever bed you want. I'm going to get this off my face and throw it in the trash." She pushed open the door to the bathroom and winced at the sight of her face.

Her left eye was swollen and red, and a bruise was forming along her jaw. Needing to take stock of all her injuries, she whipped off her hoodie and the baggy tee beneath it. A vaguely boot-shaped bruise darkened along her ribs. Honestly, she was lucky none of them had broken. The angle of hiding under the desk had worked in her favor.

Applying Vaseline around the edges of her fake beard, Violet slowly peeled it off. She tossed it into the garbage can, then looked behind her at the shower. Damn, she needed to get the grime off her. She wanted to wash the syndicate off her skin and out of her hair.

"Wanna share?" She turned back to the doorway with a gasp to see Jon leaning against the frame, watching her face.

Her first instinct was to cover her chest but Violet refrained. He'd seen it all now. "Sure. Why not?" She turned her back and dropped her jeans and briefs. Violet couldn't wait to go back to her own clothes. She was going to wear her sexiest lacy sets for a week.

With a turn of the dial, hot water pulsed through the shower head and the room started to fill with steam. Violet just stood under the hot spray, watching Jon strip through the opening in the shower curtain. Then he stepped into the shower and she moved away to let him get under the water as well. His gaze felt like a caress as he cataloged all her injuries, the same as she had. "Did you pick which bed you want?"

"Yours," he said simply. "If you're okay with sharing that, too."

Violet gulped. She couldn't think of anything she wanted more. But was that a good idea? "Jon... are you sure about that?"

He poured body wash into his hands and rubbed them together to create a lather. Then he gently began to wash her. "Why wouldn't I be?"

This had to be the absolute worst time for this conversation. "I have to go back to Virgina. I don't... do this."

His hands paused over her hips, suspicious green eyes looking up at her, and spoke with a cautious tone. "What do you mean?"

"I mean..." She grabbed a washcloth and put more soap on it, stepping as far away from him as she could in the too-small shower. "My career has always come first for me, especially when I have to be undercover for a story. It's too much to juggle what I do and a love life." She scrubbed away, not looking at him.

"I've seen too many reporters lose out on their best stories because of jealous wives or husbands." She thought of Mark, his story abandoned as he tried to reconcile with his wife. "Long hours mean unhappy spouses. You can't always control when you're going to get your big break and you miss things. Evil doesn't take a day off or care about the holidays, and if we're going to expose it, we need to be available." She washed her hair in the stony silence, then rinsed off under the warm spray. When she finally turned to look at him, he was leaning against the tiled wall, his arms crossed over his chest.

Her throat tightened and she put a hand against the wall for balance. "I'm sorry, Jon." They stared at each other for several long moments, then Violet slid the shower curtain back and stepped into the bathroom.

She shivered at the colder air, drying off quickly. The only upside to having cut her hair crazy short was how little drying time it needed. She hadn't used a blow dryer since starting at the syndicate. But she hated going to bed with a wet head, so she took advantage of the one that was built into the bathroom wall.

Jon turned off the water and stepped out of the shower. His words were devoid of emotion.

"Wanda dropped your laptop off with Roger. He brought it from Baltimore."

"Really?" She called out over the motor. It took all of five minutes to finish her hair. Growing it out was going to be a pain. "I thought you lived in Annapolis."

"Not anymore." He came up behind her and watched her face in the mirror. "I moved to Baltimore and rented a house until I find one that I want to buy."

"Why?"

"It was time to come home." He shrugged as he toweled off. She averted her eyes and booked it into the bedroom to get dressed for bed.

A sardonic chuckle followed her from the bathroom door. "At least I know it isn't me."

"What isn't you?" Ugh, she missed her comfy underwear. But Victor's boxer briefs were better than nothing.

"You're telling me, 'It's not you, it's me.' Or rather, your job. Your career." He slapped his towel onto the floor and stalked over to her as she pulled pajama pants up her legs. "I can't decide if this is better than ghosting me or not."

Great. He was having a mantrum. She pulled her t-shirt over her head and spun around to see him pulling his jeans back on. "Just spit it out, Jon."

He left her hanging, slowly getting dressed in his street clothes again. Silence descended over the room, the only sound the hum of the heater. Finally, as he was putting his wallet into his pocket along with his room key, he turned to her.

"Your job won't keep you warm at night, Violet. Your articles are important, world-changing even. But they won't cook you dinner or hold you when you have a shitty day. Eventually you won't be able to do the job this way, and you'll have to go into management or retire. One day you'll wake up and realize while you were busy running after a dream, you forgot to live."

The door clicked as he pulled it open. "Where are you going?" erupted from her mouth without her thinking about it.

He paused. "I'm going to the hotel bar. Take whichever bed you want." Then it shut behind him.

Violet rubbed at an ache behind her breastbone, but it didn't ease. No way she was going to sleep, now. Why couldn't he understand? She was doing this so he didn't get hurt.

Her gaze landed on her laptop bag. So, Roger'd had her bag in the truck, and Jon had brought it in. Unzipping the compartments, she found her actual cell phone. Not the burner she'd lost at the syndicate. Her real phone.

She fell into the desk chair and turned it on for the first time in weeks. It'd take her forever to get through all her notifications. But she bypassed them all to call the one person she knew she could count on — her brother.

He picked up on the second ring. "Biiiiiiiiitch, do you know what time it is?"

She grimaced. "I'm sorry, Cal. It's been a long ass day."

Rustling indicated he was up and ready to talk. "You're lucky I love you. What was the story this time?"

"Oh my God, Cal. It was... insane." She proceeded to give him a very condensed version of what she'd uncovered at Nautical Transit. He knew better than to tell anyone about it before she'd published the story; oftentimes rehashing events helped her figure out how to organize her thoughts. When she mentioned Jon, however, he made her stop.

"Back up, back up. You knew this guy?"

"Yeah, we met when I was undercover working on the bar with the drug ring."

"And he still came after your ass?"

"Yeah, why?"

A low whistle. "Girl, wife him up."

Violet rolled her eyes. "You know I don't do relationships."

"And I still don't understand why."

She pinched the bridge of her nose. Why had she called him again? "Because this is my dream job, and it destroys relationships." She sighed. "Remember our promise to Mom?"

"Vivi, you can't let Mom's decisions color your life like this." He'd dropped the teasing tone.

"He made her give up on her education! On her dreams!"

Callum groaned. "I need coffee for this conversation. Hold please." She could hear his feet slap against the hardwood floors in his tiny New York City apartment. It only took about ten steps before the Keurig she'd bought him for Christmas one year turned on.

After listening to him doctor his mug, he took a loud sip and then spoke once more. "You probably forgot but I was there when you asked her about that."

"What?" Violet's thoughts froze. "What are you talking about?"

Another loud sip. "I was coming into the room when you asked her why she stayed with Dad."

Holy shit. She'd nearly forgotten about asking her mom about that long ago conversation where her father had refused her request to return to classes.

"Why would you stay?"

Mom shook her head and propped her feet up after her shift at the diner. "It would have only made our lives hard, Vi. You and Callum were so young. As it turned out, I didn't have much time left with him anyway."

"But your dreams..."

"I loved your father, and I always will. He had his reasons, which we didn't get into that night, because I didn't like

to argue in front of you kids. And I can't say that having a college degree right now wouldn't make our lives easier. But I can say I'd regret spending the time on night classes when you were little, especially when he had limited time left. If I had fought him on it, I'd regret not spending that time as a family." She'd smiled then. "Love is priceless, Vi. And there are no guarantees in life. When you find it, grab a hold of it and don't let go."

Violet's brain had gone offline. "He doesn't... he can't... Cal he barely knows me!"

Callum let her sit with her thoughts for a moment. "You said he read all your articles."

"Yeah."

"And he volunteered for a dangerous mission to find you when you went AWOL."

"Um, yeah."

"Has he said anything about wanting more with you?"

"Er, well..."

"What did he say?"

She gulped. "He said, 'When I look at you, I see foreve r.'"

Callum's mug hit what sounded like his breakfast bar. "And you're saying he doesn't love you? Violet Marie Contessa Giordano!"

Shit, when Callum pulled out her middle *and* confirmation names it was serious.

"Let me guess. You shut him down without talking about what a relationship with you would look like."

"We talked about it!" She cried indignantly. "I told him evil doesn't take holidays and I have to be available."

"That sounds like you shutting him down. You mean to tell me you didn't even *consider* the idea?"

"I... Cal, I can't. I can't give this up."

"Does he want you to?"

She couldn't answer him.

The silence dragged on, and that was enough of an answer for her brother. "Look, talk to the guy. Like, actually have a conversation. And Vivi, I hope you discover that you can have more than one dream."

She swallowed around the lump in her throat. Could she?

"You know my Gemini ass couldn't make up his mind. That's why I do drag as well as fashion. But guess what? I want to find a man, too. And this dream man is going to support my other dreams, and I'll support his. Because that's what couples do. Mom didn't have any regrets. Don't you want to be able to say the same?"

"I... I'll think about it."

Cal grunted. "You do that. I'm going to order breakfast and get to work on this gown for the Met gala. Since my sister woke me up at the ass crack of dawn today."

"Love, you Cal."

His tone gentled. "Love you, too. Vivi. Let me know how it goes. And don't you chicken out."

"Damn it. You know me too well." She smiled as he barked a laugh.

"Of course I do. You sound exhausted, get some rest."

They said their goodbyes and she hung up the phone. Then she lay down in the bed with nothing but her swirling thoughts for company.

Chapter 21

Jon muttered a curse under his breath in front of the double doors that led to the hotel bar. The inside was dark, and the closed sign hung at eye level. When he checked the hours against his phone, he smacked himself in the forehead. It was four in the morning, and the bar had closed at two.

Clearly he wasn't going to sleep tonight. Thankfully Roger had offered to drive him back in the morning. Violet's car was still at the warehouse and the plan was to drop her off there. He'd intended to invite her back to Baltimore with them. But she'd never intended to stay.

He rubbed a hand over the ache in his chest and wandered back toward the lobby. There was no point going back to the room now. The last thing Jon wanted to do was fight with the woman he loved. Even if she didn't love him back.

A television playing infomercials droned on low in the background. The lobby wasn't empty. The undercover agent that he'd known as Jameson, Graham, was lounging on the couch looking as worn out as Jon felt.

"Hey man."

Graham looked up at Jon's greeting. "Hey."

"Mind if I join you?"

"Be my guest." Luke waved his hand and Jon took the arm chair next to him.

"Hell of a night."

"Yep. How's your girl?"

Jon's brows furrowed. "She's made it clear she's not my girl."

Luke snorted. "Yeah, right. She went straight to you when the chips came down."

He shook his head. "We had a thing years ago, and she ghosted me. I want to start over, and she's not interested."

"Let me guess," Luke leaned forward, his elbows on his knees. "She can't because of her job."

"You know her?" Jon's stomach dropped as he considered how that could have happened.

Luke shook his head. "Nah, but I'm in a similar line of work. It's brutal on families. I haven't been home in months."

"You got a family?"

"Just my mom and my brother now. I've tried relationships, they don't survive an undercover job. Could you go no contact with her for months at a time, not knowing if she was safe?"

"Dude, I was in the Navy. I can't tell you how many times I was cut off from my family like that."

Luke shrugged. "Yeah, but when you're the one that's left behind, it's different. Or so my exes told me." He chortled. "She's going to know that, and she's going to push you away no matter how she feels."

"You're saying I should forget her?" Jon's tone rose in indignation. How could he forget the one that got away? Forget this brave, badass woman that dove into danger to seek justice with her pen? Impossible.

"You're the only one that can decide if you can handle that life, man. She's not going to give up her job for you."

"Of course not." Jon sputtered. "Why the hell should she?"

"Did you tell her that?"

"I..." Hadn't he? When he told her how amazing he thought she was for writing these stories.

"I guess not in so many words."

Luke leaned back and eyed him up. "Let me tell you what's happened to me. I date a girl, she wants to get serious, but when work gets in the way, she wants me to quit. She doesn't like that I put myself in danger, or that I'm not at her beck and call every weekend. She hates that I can't call every night when I'm away." Luke shook his head. "Your Violet is thinking that's what's going to happen to her."

Jon shook his head in disbelief. "I never said anything of the sort."

"But you didn't say not to quit. Did you?"

The penny finally dropped, and Jon understood. "Shit."

Glass sliding doors opened up to reveal two buffet lines. A hotel employee ran around turning on the chafing dishes for the hot continental breakfast that would be ready in an hour. Percolators bubbled as the coffee brewed. Together they watched as pastries were slotted into the dispenser, waffle batter prepared and set out in pitchers, and the chafing dishes filled with bacon, sausage, and eggs. Bowls of fruit appeared over trays of ice and a trickle of sleepy guests wandered down for their morning meal.

Jon's stomach growled, He'd need his energy to get through the conversation coming with Violet.

Luke seemed to have the same idea he did, standing with him as soon as the buffet was open. "Look, I'm not her, so I can't tell you what she's thinking. But I hope that gave you some ideas."

He nodded and clapped Luke on the shoulder. "You were a huge help. Thanks, man."

AFTER EATING A BREAKFAST fit for a king, he fixed a plate for Violet and carried it upstairs, along with a tiny carton of orange juice. He needed a peace offering after storming out.

Getting back into the room without dropping something was tricky, but he managed it. The light was still on, but Violet bolted upright in bed when he came in.

"Shit, I fell asleep."

"I'm glad one of us did." He laid the plate on the desk with the silverware and juice. "I wasn't sure if you liked waffles so I got some of everything."

She shook her head and slowly slid out of bed. "You... brought me breakfast?"

Jon shrugged. She'd always looked so cute when she'd just woken up, but he looked away. He didn't feel he had the right to witness her adorableness right now. "The bar was closed when I got down there."

Violet slid into the desk chair and started cutting into her waffle. "It looks great. Thank you."

"It was the least I could do after I yelled at you last night."

She sighed as she brought the first bite up to her mouth. "Pull that armchair over and sit. Talk to me. Not at me."

He did as she requested, sitting on the edge of the cushion, right across from her. They couldn't escape each other now. "What do you want me to say?"

She cut up the rest of her waffle. "What are you expecting out of this? What do you want?"

Finally, they were getting somewhere. "I want *you*, Vee." How much clearer could he get?

Violet rolled her eyes. "As what? Your girlfriend? Wife? I work long hours and get sucked into a story, have to interview people at weird times of day. It's not conducive to having kids and running them to soccer practice."

Jon scrunched his face up. "Kids? Who said anything about kids?"

She swallowed the bite of waffle in her mouth and tilted her head at him. "You don't want kids?"

He shook his head. "I had a vasectomy years ago. I got three siblings, one of them can give my parents grandchildren. I want to be the fun uncle that hypes them up on sugar, puts them on the merry-go-round, and then gives them back."

Violet's fork clattered to the desk, her mouth agape. "R-really?"

Jon leaned forward with his elbows on his thighs. "Vee, what's really holding you back?

Her chest rose and fell with her breaths as he stared into her wide brown eyes. This was the moment of truth. Could he ever be wanted for more than a good time?

VIOLET'S EARS RANG AS she sat there, stunned. He didn't want kids? Didn't expect her to be a baby machine as the song said? Well, in for a penny, as Mom always said. It'd be better to put this out there before she got any deeper in this... whatever this was turning out to be. "I'm not giving up my career, so don't go into this thinking you can talk me out of working."

His face wrinkled up in confusion. "Why would you give up your career? Vee, you're amazing and I'm not going to get in your way. I'd like for you to be a bit safer in the future, but I can't wait to read what you write about this."

All the wind went out of her sails and her arms fell to her sides. "Really? Are you sure about that?"

Jon stood from the chair and came around the desk. "I'm not intimidated by a woman with ambition, baby."

His Adam's apple bobbed as he swallowed. "I'll take whatever you can give me. Whatever you want, Vee. I – I love you."

Her mind went blank, that one sentence swirling around and around her mind. "You... you do?"

"I have for a while." His tongue darted out to wet his lips as he ducked his chin, hesitant. "We can play this however you want. Just... don't disappear on me again. Please."

She let out a breath. Love, huh? She'd never had feelings for any of the few guys she'd dated like this. He'd come after her and saved her. He didn't want to change her. Jon just loved her.

Her mom's voice reverberated through her head once more. *"Love is priceless. When you find it, don't let go."*

Not all men were like her father. Violet felt like her whole world had just been flipped upside down, and she'd never been happier to be wrong.

Could he be any more perfect? She laughed, partly from relief and partly from fatigue, and stood up from the chair and into his arms. "I love you too, Navy boy. What the hell? Let's give this a shot."

He threaded her hair through his fingers and pulled her mouth to his. "Sounds like a plan."

Chapter 22

Finally, *finally*, Jon got his girl. The one that got away was back in his arms to stay.

He should probably let her up for air. But her lips were too enticing and she tasted divine. Jon scooped her up and her legs wrapped around his waist as he carried her into the bedroom. He laid her on the first bed, then his mouth traveled the length of her neck, his hands holding himself up over her.

"Are you still good with no condoms?"

"Yeah," she breathed. "I don't ever want to go back."

Fuck, neither did he. "Done." They each made quick work of their clothes, then his hands roamed over her lithe body as his mouth descended on hers again. He didn't need air. Just Violet. He backed her up to the bed and laid her down on the mattress. Then he kissed down her neck, nibbling at her collarbone, and continued down. She arched her back as he nipped at her breasts, sucking on her nipples one by one. He slipped his hand between her legs, drawing his finger through the moisture he found there. "Ohhh, yes," she moaned.

"Check out isn't until eleven." Roger wouldn't expect them to leave until then. He withdrew from her tits and kneeled on the floor. "And I haven't eaten this pussy in too damn long."

"Wha?" she asked as he lifted her by the ass and placed her thighs on his shoulders.

First, he licked his lips, and then he licked hers. Repeatedly. Up and down, her juices wetting his chin. Then he opened her up with his thumbs and really dove in. Her hips thrust against his face as he fucked her on his tongue. Then he slid two fingers inside and wrapped his lips around her engorged clit. He made the 'come hither' motion with his fingers and sucked her nub at the same time, and she detonated all over his face.

He was prepared to eat her out for hours, but Violet pushed him away. "Too much," she panted. "Fuck me, please."

Jon made a big show of licking his face and she groaned. Then he flipped her onto her stomach and gave her ass a light slap.

"Fuck!"

He grabbed her by the hips and slid home, her warm wet pussy enveloping him in paradise. Jon breathed slowly, trying not to explode right away. Then he leaned over and braced himself above her head.

"Say you're mine, Vee."

"You're mine." She looked back at him with a mischievous smirk.

"Damn straight I am. And you're all mine." Unable to hold back anymore, Jon rose and gripped her hips, then set a pounding pace.

"Yes! Don't stop." She buried her face in the pillow to muffle her screams.

"Never." A telltale tingle at the base of his spine told Jon he was getting close. Too close. That's when he lifted her by the shoulders and set her on her knees, his arms banded around her to hold her up.

"Oh my God!" She threw her head back against him, ecstasy was written all over her face. "I'm gonna come!"

"Come for me, Vee." He slipped one hand down and rubbed circles over her clit. "Come for your man."

She screamed, and her pussy clenched down on his cock like a vise. "Fuck! Vee!" Heat blasted from him as he filled her, his hips stuttering as he fucked her through their orgasms.

Neither one moved. His come was dripping back onto him but he didn't care one bit. Once she'd caught her breath, Violet picked up a towel from where it lay on the floor next to the bed and handed it to him. He cleaned them both up then tossed it on the bathroom floor.

Taking Violet by the hand, he pulled down the covers and slid into bed. Neither one of them bothered with getting dressed, and he pulled her into his arms where she made a pillow of his chest.

"We can't fall asleep. We need to be ready to leave with your brother."

Jon groaned at the reminder. "I just wanted to hold you." Her weight and warmth in his arms felt so right.

"I've missed this," she murmured, almost a whisper.

"I've missed you," he countered, pressing his lips to her hair. "Is there anything else you need for your story?"

Violet slapped her forehead. "I didn't get to interview the captives. Damn it!"

Jon's hands glided gently over her shoulders and back, enjoying her soft skin. "I don't think they'd have talked to you anyway. They wouldn't know which way was up yet."

He hoped the FBI got them the help they needed. Josie had been lucky, getting rescued by his brother's team. "But I have someone else that might."

"Who?"

"Josie. My brother said as long as you keep her name out of it, she'd probably be willing to talk about her experience. I have to call and ask him if he talked to her about it. But she's far enough away from the ordeal that I think she could speak to you."

Her relief was palpable. "That would be great."

He kissed her forehead. Fuck, now he could finally touch her. No way could he keep his hands off her for more than five minutes. "Where do you live in Virginia?"

"Gainesville. It's a nice little community outside D. C., where I can get to the InVestigate offices easily." D.C.? Baltimore was two hours away on a good day.

The gears in his mind whirled. "You go in every day?"

Violet snorted. "No, only when I have to. My job's almost fully remote."

He hummed. "I'd love for you to move in with me."

"But you wanted to work with your brother." She rose on her elbow to look down at his face. Jon just grinned." And? We're not that far from D. C. in Baltimore. We can keep both places and just go between them whenever you need to be in the office."

"Huh. I guess that... that sounds good." She lay back down in his arms, then peeked at the clock. "Shit, I better get ready to go."

"Finish your breakfast first." She slid out of bed and he took the opportunity to smack her perky ass cheek. She squealed and swatted his hand away.

"Better get packing, Navy boy."

"Yes, ma'am."

At least life would never be boring with his girl.

"Hi, Josie. It's so nice to meet you," Violet sat down on Jon's couch, her recording app ready on her phone. "Do you mind if I record this just for my own purposes? I wouldn't want to misquote you."

"Sure, that's fine." Josie was younger than Violet, in her twenties, and she'd endured what Violet would consider to be hell on Earth. Her blonde hair dusted her shoulders and she had the glow of a woman who'd just been on vacation.

"Do you want me to stay, Sunshine?" Finn, Jon's younger brother, hovered by the couch. The former Marine was handsome as hell, a baby face that made him look as young as Josie. The light on his bionic arm winked at her.

"I'll be fine, Finn." Josie blew him a kiss but Finn hesitated.

"Hey, Finn! Come outside with me. The landlord said I can put in a fire pit and I wanted your opinion."

"Sure. Be right there." He leaned over and gave Josie a kiss that made Violet want to fan her face. Then he followed Jon out the back door and left them alone.

Violet whistled. "You have to tell me that story after we're done with this part."

Josie laughed. "Would you believe he was my patient?"

"Really?""Yeah. It wasn't official or anything but someone wasn't taking care of his amputation right and Roger asked me to help since I had training."

"Are you sure you're okay to talk without him?"

Josie nodded her head. "I don't need to upset him by rehashing everything. He knows most of this, but I keep the details private."

Violet chuckled. "These Hunt men and their overprotective natures, huh?"

"Exactly!" Josie said with a grin.

"Alright, let me get the recording started." Violet hit a button. She rattled off the time and date, then used Finn's nickname for Josie to inspire her code name. "This is Sunny, a survivor of the human trafficking ring run by the organization known as the syndicate. Sunny, tell me in your own words, how you came to be a part of this ring."

The name must have put that grin on her face, because Josie spun her a tale of an abusive deadbeat ex-boyfriend that she'd been planning to leave, who'd allowed her to be kidnapped in exchange for money. She recounted some of her harrowing experiences as a captive and explained in detail the deplorable conditions they'd lived in.

Hours later, after the sun had set, and the boys had gone down to the basement to watch a movie in what Jon called his "man cave", Violet had more than what she needed for the article. She stopped the recording, noticing how low her battery was. "Josie, I give you all the credit. I couldn't have survived the way you did."

"You don't know that. I never would have thought that before it became my life."

Violet's energy had drained just listening to her. "You know, you could write one hell of a memoir. The talk show hosts would be clamoring to get you on their stages."

Josie shook her head vehemently. "I'm no writer. And I'm pretty sure people would think it was fiction." She wrapped her arms around herself. "Besides, I want to put it behind me. And knowing the FBI finally caught these guys, now I can."

Violet smiled. Of course, a private person like Josie wouldn't want to capitalize on her story, no matter how well it might sell. "If you ever reconsider, I'd do the writing for you."

"Thanks," Josie gave her a tight smile. "But I doubt it."

"That's fair." She stood and stretched. "Shall we go see what the boys are up to?"

"Sounds like a great idea. I'm starving."

Chapter 23

IT WAS A CELEBRATION at the Hunt Security Headquarters, which was what Jon had affectionately started calling his older brother's house. Violet had spent just as much time here getting to know Jenna, Frankie, and Josie as she had at Jon's house. She'd all but moved out of her small condo in Gainesville, leaving a few office-ready outfits and her furniture behind for when she had to be in town.

Wanda had been thrilled when she finally turned in her finished article. She had run it as a series across three issues of InVestigate, due to the sheer length. And she'd hinted more than once that she'd sent it to some awards programs, though which ones she didn't say.

The highly televised trial over the last several months had captured everyone's attention. Every last member of the syndicate and their customers had been exposed and charged with a litany of crimes. The lists that Frankie had turned out from the syndicate servers had caused mass upheavals in all levels of government, exposing corruption nationwide. It had become a huge media circus with a laundry list of defendants, both celebrities and politicians being exposed as customers or accessories. The number of special elections going on was unprecedented. Corporate America was in turmoil as CEOs and presidents got ousted by their shareholders. Even if this verdict didn't go their way tonight, the court of public opinion had already declared them guilty. Frankie hadn't stopped grinning since the article hit.

It was glorious to watch these people get their comeuppance.

Victims were still coming out of the woodwork. There was a whole network of therapists signed up to treat them through a nonprofit, since most of the victims had no insurance.

Today the jury had finally announced they were done deliberating the case against the twelve men in charge of the organization. Most of the lower echelon had accepted plea deals for a lesser sentence, but these men would get no such deal. The country wanted justice.

Violet felt bad for the people who got picked to be on the jury. They'd endured weeks of gut-wrenching testimony.

The four couples were gathered around Roger's living room where his flatscreen glowed up on the wall. Violet bit at her nail. The judge on the screen called for order.

"People of the jury, how do you find?"

"Guilty on all counts, Your Honor."

A cheer went up that drowned out the news correspondent on the screen. Finn rocked a tearful Josie back and forth in his arms. Frankie punched the air, then high-fived Jenna. Roger disappeared to the kitchen and returned with a bottle of champagne.

Jon laughed. "Roger, do you even have champagne glasses?"

"I got these special." He went back into the kitchen and Jenna followed, the two of them returning with four flute glasses each. "Jon, pop the cork."

Violet grinned as Jon did, and they cheered again as the bubbly spilled in an arc, mostly into the glasses Roger had placed on the coffee table. He poured the glasses full and then set the bottle back down.

Roger picked up a glass and raised it. "A toast. To all of you. And an amazing job."

"To Hunt Security," chimed in Jon.

"To brotherhood." Sam clinked his glass with theirs.

"To freedom," said Josie, wiping her eyes.

"To justice!" Jenna and Frankie said at the same time.

"To... oh shit, that's Wanda's ringtone." Violet fished her phone out of her pocket and slid the green button to accept it. "Hi, Wanda. Did you see the news?"

"I did but I have even better news for you!"

Violet stood there awkwardly with her champagne in one hand and her phone in the other. "I'm kinda in the middle of celebrating here, what's up?"

"Well, celebrate harder, missy! You're a finalist for the Pulitzer Prize!"

Violet's jaw dropped and she fumbled her phone. Jon saved it and held it out to her. She hit the speaker phone button. "Say that again?"

"Your article on the syndicate is a finalist for the Pulitzer! I'm so proud of you! But you're not allowed to disappear on me again, you hear?"

"I... I can't caldeive it."

"Believe it! Alright, I'll let you get back to whatever you're doing. You've earned it!" Then Wanda hung up, and Violet looked around at the faces grinning at her. And Jon absolutely glowed with pride.

She opened her mouth to speak and then shut it again. Twice. "I... I have no words."

"To Violet!" Jon toasted, and the rest of them echoed him.

He kissed her after they'd taken their drinks, and nothing was sweeter than champagne on his lips.

ACROSS MARYLAND, LUKE GRAHAM sat with a beer and watched the verdict announcement on his recliner with only half of his attention. Because what kept dragging his focus away from the television was the letter from his mother in his hands.

He'd told her he'd be out of contact for a while, and that had turned into months of undercover work. He'd paused his mail and he was glad he had. Once he reinstated it, and went to the post office to pick it up, he had sifted through all of the junk to find an envelope from his hometown of Hawthorn Hills, Pennsylvania.

Knowing she couldn't reach him by phone, Mom had gone old-school.

While the news correspondent droned on about the implications of the verdict of the case that Luke had worked his ass off for, he read her familiar handwriting once more.

My dearest Luke,

I know I can't reach you by phone and I have no idea when you'll get this letter. But Aaron is acting strange and I don't know what to do. Ever since your father died, he's been acting out, but now that he's out of school it's gotten so much worse. He's out at all hours of the night, he sleeps all day, and he won't tell me where he's going, what he's doing, or who he's with. I know he's eighteen now and an adult, but a mother worries. He refuses to get a job, but he's buying video games and fancy watches. Where is he getting the money? Nothing of mine has gone missing. I suppose I should be grateful that he's earning it somehow, but I don't believe it's legitimate. And the way he talks to me! Your father would have beaten him, but I don't have the heart.

There's been talk around town of kids overdosing on drugs. Just last week Suzy's Michael had to go to the hospital and while Suzy refuses to talk about it, the word is he got high on something. Some people say it was crack cocaine and some say it was heroin. You don't think Aaron is involved in drugs, do you? Not my sweet boy. Although ever since Dad died, he hasn't been all that sweet.

When you get done with your assignment, please call me. Maybe you could come home for a visit? Aaron could use a positive male influence around here for a bit.

Stay safe.

Love,

Mom

Luke flipped the letter over in his hands, a plan forming. He muted the television and picked up his phone. It was evening, and Mom would be at the church for bingo night, but he left her a voicemail, anyway.

"Hi Mom, it's Luke. I'm coming home."

JON BLINKED BACK TEARS from his eyes again as they threw bird seed at Nadia and Caleb while they walked down the steps to the church. His baby sister was married. Jon had never seen her so happy. Caleb cleaned up nicely in his tuxedo, and she looked elegant and grown up as fuck in her ivory ballgown. Her four friends wore hunter green dresses and carried bouquets filled with fall flowers. Baltimore had turned out its finest colors for her October wedding photos and he couldn't wait to see them.

The limo for the bridal party stood idling down on the street, but in front of the steps was a familiar gunmetal gray motorcycle. Someone had tied cans on strings to the exhaust pipe.

"Is Caleb really going to ride his bike to the venue?" Jon leaned over and whispered to Finn.

Finn shrugged. Then one of Nadia's friends approached and handed her a white helmet. Nadia threw her head back and laughed. In light blue letters, the back of the helmet said "Just Married."

Mom's jaw dropped. "Nadia Lynn, you are not riding on that in your wedding dress!"

"I sure am!" With that, Nadia ripped at her waist and her big skirt came flying off to reveal a white jumpsuit underneath.

Jon and Finn both bent over laughing. Violet and Josie looked confused. Vee tapped him on the shoulder. "I don't get it. What's so funny?"

He tried to catch his breath as Jade, the tall deep-skinned bridesmaid who he vaguely remembered being good at sewing, caught the skirt and folded it over her arm. "Nadia hates dresses." He turned to Jade. "Whose idea was that?"

She beamed. "Mine. Mama Hunt kept insisting, and Nad hated every single gown. So, I convinced her to do the skirt for the ceremony and pictures, but she'd be completely comfortable underneath. Judy had no idea when she came out in the 'dress' that it was actually pants and a skirt."

"You're a genius." Jon shook his head while Finn clapped and cheered as their baby sister hopped on Caleb's bike and threw her bouquet at the stairs.

Right into Olivia's arms.

Jade chuckled. "A little out of order, but like hell was Nad doing a garter."

"I'm pretty sure Caleb would have had three brothers trying to rip his arms off, wedding or no," Violet mused.

"You're not wrong, love." He leaned over and kissed her as Nadia's friends squealed over Olivia catching the bouquet. "Let's get Mom to the reception before she has a stroke."

Finn chuckled. "That's probably a good idea."

The party went on into the night and Jon was grateful he'd already checked them into the hotel. All they had to do was go to the elevator and head up to their room.

Violet fell back against the white bedspread, her dark hair fanning out around her like a halo. Her hair was longer now, a cute little bob. He liked her with any amount of hair, though he thought the longer style suited her best.

"My feet feel like they're going to fall off."

"Here, baby, let me get your shoes." He'd been looking forward to the heels of those sexy, strappy sandals digging into his back as he ate her out, but her comfort was more important. Kneeling on the floor next to the bed, he lifted her foot up to his shoulder and carefully worked the tiny strap through the buckle. She moaned as her foot slipped free. He left her foot up there while he did the same to the other, then sat cross-legged on the floor and rubbed them gently.

"That feels amazing."

"You were awesome out there."

"I didn't get to go dancing much in my twenties. I kinda wish I had."

He smiled up at her. "Too busy building your career?"

"Yeah, and I felt guilty partying when my mom was so sick. So, I focused on school because I felt like that's what she wanted."

He'd have to ask around, and see where was good, but he'd take her dancing more. Jon had loved watching her have the time of her life on the floor tonight. "We still got time."

"True." She propped herself up on her hands and grinned down at him. "You shocked your sister and her friends with your dance moves."

He threw his head back and laughed, the surprised looks on their faces flitting through his memory. "Nadia was so young when I was learning those, she wouldn't remember it."

"I remember the first time I saw you break them out at the Nail. Most guys think dancing is for girls."

He snorted. "Did you see Sam and Frankie out there tonight? Apparently, he took ballroom lessons as a kid."

"I can believe it. They looked phenomenal." Violet let out a little yawn. "I need a shower."

"That sounds like an excellent idea." He waggled his eyebrows. Violet tried to toss a pillow at his head, but her arm flopped down like it was too much energy.

"I am too exhausted for all that."

"What if I hold you up against the wall?"

That made her pause, and Jon knew he had piqued her interest.

"I could be convinced."

Jon had never stripped down so fast in his life. She sat up and struggled with her zipper until he freed her from her dark purple dress. The sweetheart neckline had been teasing him all night with her cleavage, and he needed his mouth on her hours ago.

Once they were both naked, Jon picked her up and carried her into the bathroom, setting her on the counter next to the sink while he started the water running. As steam filled the room, he lifted her up again.

"I can walk, you know."

"But your feet hurt. Let me do this."

"They're much better without the shoes."

"Hush, woman."

She rolled her eyes as she always did when he went caveman on her. At least he could admit when he was doing it. He set her down when they got inside the spray. She caught him ogling more than once while she lathered up, and then when she started to rinse, he hurried through his own routine. Then he kissed her under the rainfall showerhead, his hands running over her lithe body. She kissed him back with fervor, and when her hands went around his neck, he grabbed her ass and hoisted her up in line with his cock.

"Damn, you were serious."

"Always am about you." He slanted his mouth over hers once more and pressed his tongue inside in a tease of what he was about to do to her pussy.

She groaned and broke the connection again. "I can't wait. Get inside me."

"As you wish." Jon sucked in a breath as he entered her, every time like the first time he got inside her bare. Her heat welcomed him and she wrapped her legs around his waist as he pressed her against the wall and started to fuck her hard like she loved.

Violet threw her head back against the tile. "Yes! Right there! Don't stop!" Never. He'd never stop. Fucking her, loving her. Wanting her. He'd never get enough.

It wasn't long before she came the first time, but he held on and fucked her through it. She latched her mouth onto his as he drove toward his own climax, her whimpers and moans giving him life. A tingle moved up from his toes to the base of his spine, and when her pussy spasmed a second time, he came with her. Stars erupted behind his eyes, and he slowed down, the water rinsing away any evidence.

He held a sleepy, satisfied Violet in his arms, her eyes glazed over in the afterglow. Jon figured he looked about the same. "God, I love you," she slurred.

"I love you, too. Let's go to bed."

He turned off the water and toweled them off, even helping Violet dry her hair when her arms proved to be too weak to hold up the hairdryer. Then he bundled her up in bed, and turned out the lights, sliding in behind her.

"We should get one of those shower heads."

"You mean when we buy a house?" Jon was definitely not interested in sleep now. He'd been dropping hints for months about them buying a house together. He figured she was less likely to run if he talked about that than if he started talking about rings.

"Yeah." She nodded once and then her breathing evened out, and he knew she was asleep.

Mentally he punched the air. She was finally thinking about their future. In reality, he snuggled in behind his girl and willed himself to go to sleep. If he started dreaming of a big walk-in shower with a built-in bench, no one would know.

Epilogue

FLAMES CRACKLED IN ROGER'S fire pit, the sounds of his woods at night surrounding them. The full moon rose in the sky and the stars were peeking out from their daytime shrouds. Wrapped in hoodies and huddled around the metal pit were his brothers and their women. Next to him, Jenna roasted a hot dog in the orange glow.

"Still concerned about your wiener?" She smirked at him, her red hair lit like a devilish halo.

"Not anymore. I know how much you like it." He winked and took a pull from his beer bottle. She laughed and placed her not-burnt meat into a bun and drew a line of ketchup along it.

"Pass the buns?" Frankie asked. She jumped in her chair with a squeal as Sam's eyes darted to the side and his hand drew back from her seat. "Not those buns, Soldier boy."

"But they're my favorite." He grinned.

Roger had seen Sam come so far out of his shell that their old unit probably wouldn't even recognize him some days. And it was all thanks to the hacker keeping him on his toes. She'd traded her black hat for a white one, but sometimes Roger wondered about her methods.

Josie was curled up in Finn's lap, content as a cat, his bionic arm wrapped around her shoulders as they watched the blaze. Violet and Jon were both plowing through their second hot dogs.

"I thought this was a business meeting," Finn asked from across the pit, one eyebrow raised.

"It is. But it's also a family meeting." Roger raised his bottle and gestured around. "And we need to discuss what direction we're taking Hunt Security in the future."

Jenna licked ketchup off her fingers and sat back in her camping chair. "What do you mean?"

"It's been a wild-ass year," he said. Now that he had their attention, Roger wasn't sure what to say.

"That's my fault," Frankie said. "Y'all didn't have to help me when I came here asking for help to take the syndicate down." She turned to Violet. "You getting us that decoder could have got you in a world of trouble."

"I'm grateful you did," Josie piped up. Finn's arms tightened around her. "I'm so grateful that thug knocked me out cold and couldn't get me out of the house." Her loving boyfriend kissed the top of her head, his eyes distant.

"I don't regret a single thing we've done this year," Roger declared. "But I think I'm a bit too old to go doing any more rescue missions." He shifted in his seat, his joints getting stiff from sitting around.

"Getting shot, even through the vest, was not pleasant," Sam agreed. "And to be honest we don't have the manpower to do those jobs effectively. We've been lucky fuckers."

"I'm fine sticking to regular bodyguard gigs. And the cyber side is really taking off thanks to you and Frankie." Roger raised his beer to them.

"I'm not interested in anything that takes me away overnight," Finn said, and the others nodded. "We've worked too hard not to spend time with our loved ones and our families."

"Amen to that," Jon said. "I like coming home at the end of the day."

"It's settled, then." Roger twisted until he heard his back crack, then settled back into his chair. "I'm sure Ross will be thrilled not to hear from us anymore."

"I like him and Heather, they're good people." Jenna ripped open the bag of marshmallows.

"Doesn't mean we made his job any easier." Sam chuckled.

"Hey without us, he wouldn't have been able to organize that raid!" Frankie fisted her hands on her hips.

"I'm not disagreeing with you, sweetness. But the amount of paperwork he probably had to fill out to cover his ass doubled."

"Well, you win some, you lose some." Jenna handed the bag of marshmallows to Frankie, who was making grabby hands.

They chatted well into the early hours of the morning, the fire dying into embers eventually. Sam and Frankie were traveling down to Florida for Thanksgiving to see Sam's mom and aunt. Violet's brother was to be subjected to a Hunt family holiday. She couldn't wait, and had even helped him line up a few gigs while he was down here. Roger thought perhaps she was hoping he'd move south, so they could be closer. It looked like they'd all be going to a drag show. The women were thrilled. The men not so much.

Once the flames had died down and everyone was yawning, they went back into his house. Finn and Josie were still using his spare bedroom upstairs, but not for much longer.

"I'll see you all Monday," Frankie said as she hugged Jenna good night.

"And we'll see you next weekend for the big move!" Violet hugged Josie, who sighed.

"I can't wait. Roger's been so nice about us staying here."

"House hunting isn't easy. I get it." He wrapped his arms around his pseudo sister and clapped Finn on the shoulder before giving the same farewells to Sam and Frankie. "See y'all Monday."

Their headlights drove down his gravel driveway until they couldn't see them through the trees anymore.

Josie and Finn had already gone upstairs, so Roger did his nightly security check of the windows and doors then met Jenna at the base of the stairs.

"Feeling better now that's settled?"

"Now what's settled?"

She smiled. "About the business."

"Yep. Just a nice normal security business."

His little Amazon snorted. "Nothing about us is normal."

"That does it," he said as he put his shoulder under her hips and lifted. She squealed in dismay.

"Roger!"

"Take it back."

"Never!"

Smack!

"Did you seriously just spank me?"

He smacked her ass again when he got to the top of the stairs.

"Roger!"

"Shh, Finn and Josie are trying to sleep."

She growled. God, she was adorable.

"Put me down!"

"As you wish." He flipped her over his shoulder and her back hit their mattress.

That got her to laugh. "I smell like a campfire."

Roger shrugged. "Is that supposed to be a bad thing?"

"I want a shower."

He grinned. "Let's save water."

Jenna just rolled her eyes. "No funny business. It's late as hell."

Roger didn't make any such promise.

THANK YOU SO MUCH for reading Hunt Security! Don't forget to leave a review!

And if you want to see an illustration of the stargazing scene, sign up for my newsletter!

Also By Jasmine

For a current list of my available titles, scan the QR code below:

Notes from Jasmine

Hot damn. I'm officially up to a dozen books now. It's really funny that my twelfth book was so inspired by Twelfth Night. That play is burned into my memory thanks to a guy I dated who was an actor. He was in a production of it and like the dutiful girlfriend I was, I went to see it more than once.

The dual hidden identity plot was such a fun device to work with and I hope you loved it too.

Honestly, the plot of this book went through an incredible evolution. At first I wanted the characters to play it safe, but my muse got so bored she up and left and I couldn't write for months. Thanks to my sister I got out of that first rut, outlined a new plot, and started over with what I called Rough Draft 2.0. Thousands of words later, I sent what I thought was the story to Maria Secoy, my talented critique partner. But I knew something was off; I just couldn't figure out what. She advised me the issues were in the first third of the novel, and so I rewrote the beginning *again*. (Thanks Maria!)

My amazing beta team also had lots of changes for me to make, though thankfully I didn't have to rewrite nearly as much. And then of course I sent it to Jenn, who as usual gave me some great ideas for more additions. The final product is a story I'm extremely proud of. I didn't set out to write a cathartic release of *the files* but here we are, and I'm not mad about it.

I wouldn't have made it through all these edits without H.K. Darkwood's writing sprint livestreams. (She also came up with the name of the boat, *Ridin' U Dry*. <3)

And frankly, I wouldn't have written this series at all if you, my readers, hadn't asked me for stories about Nadia's brothers. I am so sad to leave the Hunt family behind but I imagine we'll hear from them again.

I love evolving as an author and I definitely enjoy the romantic suspense space. I have no plans to leave it anytime soon. But there's another side to Jasmine coming out in Hawthorn Hills and I can't wait to get started. This town will host *two* series. I can't wait to see you there!

XOXO,

Jasmine

About the Author

I inherited my love of reading from my parents. As the daughter of two teachers, one of whom is also a librarian, I was the kid who walked out of the library with the maximum number of books each week, then walked back in the following week having read every single one. This would go on all summer long. When I could put pencil to paper, I started writing my own (terrible) kid's stories. Around age eight, I told my mom I wanted to be an author when I grew up, but she talked me out of it. She wanted me to have a stable career because of my poor health.

While I learned to manage my chronic condition through childhood, I also kept writing as a creative outlet. But when I grew up and turned my focus to my career, writing went by the wayside. The stories would not come again until quarantine in 2020 when trauma from the year before poured out of me in a cathartic story now known as *Roar for Me*. The decision to self-publish was an easy one. I consider each book its own work of art and I want to control not only what I write, but all the packaging, as well.

I write books I want to read. This means intelligent characters, happy-ever-afters, and no cheating. Adult contemporary romances with plenty of steam appeal to me the most. Music and pop culture are my biggest sources of inspiration. And I love to flip the script and surprise readers by putting a twist on their expectations.

Everyone deserves their own love story. I've always believed that. I want to develop a wide range of characters so everyone can relate to someone in one of my books. I especially love challenging gender expectations. And I hope my books will be an escape for readers, not just entertainment. When I'm not writing, I'm working in healthcare in my native Pittsburgh. Or you might find me crafting, baking sweet treats, or playing *Mario Kart* with my own nerdy love.